CH00842912

THE DAUGHTER OF THE CHIEFTAIN: THE STORY OF AN INDIAN GIRL

BY
Edward S. Ellis

FOREWORD

This is a story that chronicles the lives of several Native Americans whose paths intertwine.

CHAPTER ONE: OMAS, ALICE, AND LINNA

I don't suppose there is any use in trying to find out when the game of "Jack Stones" was first played. No one can tell. It certainly is a good many hundred years old.

All boys and girls know how to play it. There is the little rubber ball, which you toss in the air, catch up one of the odd iron prongs, without touching another, and while the ball is aloft; then you do the same with another, and again with another, until none is left. After that you seize a couple at a time, until all have been used; then three, and four, and so on, with other variations, to the end of the game.

Doubtless your fathers and mothers, if they watch you during the progress of the play, will think it easy and simple. If they do, persuade them to try it. You will soon laugh at their failure.

Now, when we older folks were young like you, we did not have the regular, scraggly bits of iron and dainty rubber ball. We played with pieces of stones. I suspect more deftness was needed in handling them than in using the new fashioned pieces. Certainly, in trials than I can remember, I never played the game through without a break; but then I was never half so handy as you are at such things: that, no doubt, accounts for it.

Well, a good many years ago, before any of your fathers or mothers were born, a little girl named Alice Ripley sat near her home playing "Jack Stones." It was the first of July, 1778, and although her house was made of logs, had no carpets or stove, but a big fireplace, where all the food was made ready for eating, yet no sweeter or happier girl can be found today, if you spend weeks in searching for her. Nor can you come upon a more lovely spot in which to build a home, for it was the famed Wyoming Valley, in Western Pennsylvania.

Now, since some of my young friends may not be acquainted with this place, you will allow me to tell you that the Wyoming Valley lies between the Blue Ridge and the Alleghany Mountains, and that the beautiful Susquehanna River runs through it.

The valley runs northeast and southwest, and is twenty-one miles long, with an average breadth of three miles. The bottom lands—that is, those in the lowest portion—are sometimes overflowed when there is an unusual quantity of water in the river. In some places the plains are level, and in others, rolling. The soil is very fertile.

Two mountain ranges hem in the valley. The one on the east has an average height of a thousand feet, and the other two hundred feet less. The eastern range is steep, mostly barren, and abounds with caverns, clefts, ravines, and forests. The western is not nearly so wild, and is mostly cultivated.

The meaning of the Indian word for Wyoming is "Large Plains," which, like most of the Indian names, fits very well indeed.

The first white man who visited Wyoming was a good Moravian missionary, Count Zinzendorf—in 1742. He toiled among the Delaware Indians who lived there, and those of his faith who followed him were the means of the conversion of a great many red men.

The fierce warriors became humble Christians, who set the best example to wild brethren, and often to the wicked white men.

More than twenty years before the Revolution settlers began making their way into the Wyoming Valley. You would think their only trouble would be with the Indians, who always look with anger upon intruders of that kind, but really their chief difficulty was with white people.

Most of these pioneers came from Connecticut. The successors of William Penn, who had bought Pennsylvania from his king, and then again from the Indians, did not fancy having settlers from other colonies take possession of one of the garden spots of his grant.

I cannot tell you about the quarrels between the settlers from Connecticut and those that were already living in Pennsylvania. Forty of the invaders, as they may be called, put up a fort, which was named on that account Forty Fort. This was in the winter of 1769, and two hundred more pioneers followed them in the spring. The fort stood on the western bank of the river.

The Pennsylvanians, however, had prepared for them, and the trouble began. During the few years following, the New Englanders were three times driven out of the valley, and the men, women, and children were obliged to tramp for two hundred miles through the unbroken wilderness to their old homes. But they rallied and came back again, and at last were strong enough to hold their ground. About this time the mutterings of the American Revolution began to be heard, and the Pennsylvanians and New Englanders forgot their enmity and became brothers in their struggle for independence.

Among the pioneers from Connecticut who put up their old fashioned log houses in Wyoming were George Ripley and his wife Ruth. They were young, frugal, industrious, and worthy people. They had but one child—a boy named Benjamin; but after awhile Alice was added to the family, and at the date of which I am telling you she was six years and her brother thirteen years old.

Mr. Ripley was absent with the continental army under General Washington, fighting the battles of his country. Benjamin, on this spring day, was visiting some of his friends further down the valley; so that when Alice came forth to play "Jack Stones" alone, no one was in sight, though her next neighbor lived hardly two hundred yards away.

I wish you could have seen her as she looked on that summer afternoon. She had been helping, so far as she was able, her mother in the house, until the parent told her to go outdoors and amuse herself. She was chubby, plump, healthy, with round pink cheeks, yellow hair tied in a coil at the back of her head, and her big eyes were as blue, and clear, and bright as they could be.

She wore a brown homespun dress—that is to say, the materials had been woven by the deft fingers of her mother, with the aid of the old spinning wheel, which in those days formed a part of every household. The dark stockings were knitted by the same busy fingers, with the help of the flashing needles; and the shoes, put together by Peleg Quintin, the humpbacked shoemaker, were heavy and coarse, and did not fit any too well.

The few simple articles of underwear were all homemade, clean, and comfortable, and the same could be said of the clothing of the brother and of the mother herself.

Alice came running out of the open front door, bounding off the big flat stone which served as a step with a single leap, and, running to a spot of green grass a few yards away, where there was not a bit of dirt or a speck of dust, she sat down and began the game of which I told you at the opening of this story.

Alice was left handed. So when she took position, she leaned over to the right, supporting her body with that arm, while with the other hand she tossed the little jagged pieces of stone aloft, snatching up the others, and letting the one that was going up and down in the air drop into her chubby palm.

She had been playing perhaps ten minutes, when she found someone was watching her.

She did not see him at first, but heard a low, deep "Huh!" partly at one side and partly behind her.

Instead of glancing around, she finished the turn of the game on which she was engaged just then. That done, she clasped all the Jack Stones in her hand, assumed the upright posture, and looked behind her.

"I thought it was you, Omas," she said with a merry laugh; "do you want to play Jack Stones with me?"

If you could have seen the person whom she thus addressed, you would have thought it a strange way of speaking.

He was an Indian warrior, belonging to the tribe of Delawares. Those who knew about him said he was one of the fiercest red men that ever went on the warpath. A few years before, there had been a massacre of the settlers, and Omas was foremost among the Indians who swung the tomahawk and fired his rifle at the white people.

He was tall, sinewy, active, and powerful. Three stained eagle feathers were fastened on his crown in the long black hair, and his hunting shirt, leggings, and moccasins were bright with different colored beads and fringes. In the red sash which passed around his waist were thrust a hunting knife and tomahawk, while one hand clasped a cumbersome rifle, which, like all firearms of those times, was used with ramrod and flintlock.

Omas would have had a rather pleasing face had he let it alone; but his people love bright colors, and he was never seen without a lot of paint daubed over it. This was made up of black, white, and yellow circles, lines, and streaks that made him look frightful.

But Alice was not scared at all. She and Omas were old friends. Nearly a year before, he stopped at their cabin one stormy night and asked for something to eat. Mrs. Ripley gave him plenty of coarse brown, well baked bread and cold meat, and allowed him to sleep on the floor until morning.

Benjamin was rather shy of the fierce looking Delaware, but Alice took to him at first. She brought him a basin of water, and asked him to please wash his face.

The startled mother gently reproved her; but Omas did that which an Indian rarely does—smiled. He spoke English unusually well, and knew why the child had proposed to him to use the water.

He told her that he had a little girl that he called Linna, about the same age as Alice. Upon hearing this, what did Alice do, but climb upon the warrior's knee and ask him to tell her all about Linna. Well, the result was, that an affection was formed between this wild warrior and the gentle little girl.

Omas promised to bring his child to see Alice, who, with her mother's permission, said she would return the visit. There can be no doubt that the Delaware often went a long way out of his course, for no other reason than to spend an hour or less with Alice Ripley. The brother and mother always made him feel welcome, and to the good parent the influence of her child upon the savage red man had a peculiar interest which nothing else in the world could possess for her. So you understand why it was that Alice did not start and show any fear when she looked around and saw the warrior standing less than ten feet off, and attentively watching her.

"You can't play Jack Stones as well as I," she said, looking saucily up at him.

"I beat you," was his reply, as he strode forward and sat down cross legged on the grass.

"I'd like to see you do it! You think you're very smart, don't you?"

A shadowy smile played around the stern mouth, and the Delaware, who had studied the simple game long enough to understand it, began the sport under the observant eyes of his little mistress.

While both were intent on the amusement, Mrs. Ripley came to the door and stood wonderingly looking at them.

"It does seem as if Indians are human beings like the rest of us," was her thought; "but who could resist her gentle ways?"

Up went the single stone in the air, and Omas grabbed the batch that were lying on the ground, and then caught the first as it came down.

"That won't do!" called Alice, seizing the brawny hand, which—sad to say—had been stained with blood as innocent as hers; "you didn't do that fair!"

"What de matter?" he asked, looking reproachfully into the round face almost against his own.

"I'll show you how. Now, I lay those three on the ground like that. Then I toss up this, pick up one without touching any of the others, keep it in my hand and pick up the next—see?"

She illustrated her instruction by her work, while her pupil listened and stared.

"I know—I know," he said quickly. "I show you." Then the wag of a Delaware tossed the first stone fully twenty feet aloft, caught up the others, and took that on the fly.

"I never saw anybody as dumb as you," was the comment. "What is the use of your trying? You couldn't learn to play Jack Stones in ever so long."

She was about to try him again, when, childlike, she darted off upon a widely different subject, for it had just come into her little head.

"Omas, when you were here the other day, you promised that the next time you came to see me you would bring Linna."

"Dat so—Omas promise."

"Then why haven't you done as you said?"

"Omas never speak with double tongue; he bring Linna with him."

"You did?—where is she?" asked Alice, springing to her feet, clasping her hands, and looking expectantly around.

The Delaware emitted a shrill, tremulous whistle, and immediately from the wood several rods behind them came running the oddest looking little girl anyone could have met in a long time.

Her face was as round as that of Alice, her long, black hair hung loosely over her shoulders, her small eyes were as black as jet, her nose a pug, her teeth as white and regular as were ever seen, while her dress was a rude imitation of her father's except the skirt came below her knees. Her feet were as small as a doll's, and encased in the beaded little moccasins, were as pretty as they could be.

"That is Linna," said the proud father as she came obediently forward.

CHAPTER TWO: DANGER IN THE AIR

Little Linna, daughter of Omas, the Delaware warrior, was of the same age as Alice Ripley. The weather was warm although she wore tiny moccasins to protect her feet, she scorned the superfluous stockings and undergarments that formed a part of the other's apparel.

Her hair was as black, abundant, and almost as long as her father's; but her face was clean, and, perhaps in honor of the occasion, she, too, sported a gaudy eagle feather in her hair.

She bounded out of the green wood like a fawn, but as she drew near her parent and Alice, her footsteps became slower, and she halted a few paces away, hung her head, with her forefinger between her pretty white teeth—for all the world like any white girl of her years.

But Alice did not allow her to remain embarrassed. She had been begging for this visit, and now, when she saw her friend, she ran forward, took her little plump hand and said—"Linna, I am real glad you have come!"

Omas had risen to his feet, and watched the girls with an affection and interest which found no expression on his painted face. His child looked timidly up to him and walked slowly forward, her hand clasped in that of Alice. She did not speak, but when her escort sat down on the grass, she did the same.

"Linna, do you know how to play Jack Stones?" asked Alice, picking up the pebbles.

Linna shook her head quickly several times, but her lips remained mute.

"Your father thought he knew how, but he don't; he doesn't play fair, either. Let me show you, so you can beat him when you go home."

Alice set to work, while the bright black eyes watched every movement.

"Now do you want to try it?" she asked, after going through the game several times.

Linna nodded her head with the same birdlike quickness, and reached out her chubby hand.

Her father and Alice watched her closely. She made several failures at first, all of which were patiently explained by her tutor; by and by she went through the performance from beginning to end without a break.

Alice clapped her hands with delight, and Omas—certain that no grownup person saw him—smiled with pleasure.

"Doesn't she know how to talk?" asked Alice, looking up at the warrior. Omas spoke somewhat sharply to his child in the Delaware tongue. She startled, and looking at Alice, asked—

"Do—yoo think me play well?"

Alice was delighted to find she could make herself understood so easily. It was wonderful how she had learned to speak English so early in life.

"I guess you can," was the ready reply of Alice; "your father can't begin to play as well. When you go home you can show your mamma how to play Jack Stones. Have you any brothers and sisters?"

"No; me have no brother—no sister."

"That's too bad! I've got a big brother Ben. He isn't home now, but he will be here to supper. He's a nice boy, and you will like him. Let's go in the house now to see mamma, and you can teach me how to talk Indian."

Both girls bounded to their feet, and hand in hand, walked to the door, with Omas gravely stalking after them.

Mrs. Ripley had learned of the visitor, and stood on the threshold to welcome her. She took her by the hand and led her inside. Omas paused, as if in doubt whether he should follow; but her invitation to him was so cordial, that he stepped within and seated himself on a chair.

That afternoon and night could never be forgotten by Alice Ripley. In a very little while she and her visitor were on the best of terms; laughing, romping, and chasing each other in and out of doors, just as if they were twin sisters that had never been separated from each other.

When Mrs. Ripley asked Omas for how long a time he could leave his child with them, he said he must take her back that evening. His wigwam was a good many miles away in the woods, and he would have to travel all night to reach the village of his tribe.

Mrs. Ripley, however, pleaded so hard, that he consented to let his child stay until he came back the next day or soon thereafter for her.

When he rose to go, the long summer day was drawing to a close. He spoke to Linna in their native tongue. She was sitting on the floor just then, playing with a wonderful rag baby, but was up in a flash, and followed him outside.

"Wait a moment and she will come back," said Mrs. Ripley to her own child. She knew what the movement meant: Omas did not wish anyone to see him and Linna.

On the outside he moved to the left, and glanced around to make sure that no person was looking that way. Then he lifted the little one from the ground; she threw her arms around his neck, and he pressed her to his breast and kissed her several times with great warmth. Then he set her down, and she ran laughing into the house, while he strode off to the woods.

But at the moment of entering them he stopped abruptly, wheeled about, and walked slowly back toward the cabin.

Upon the return of Linna, Mrs. Ripley stepped to the front door to look for her son. He was not in sight, but Omas had stopped again hardly a rod distant. He stood a moment, looking fixedly at her, and then beckoned with his free hand for her to approach.

Without hesitation she stepped off the broad flat stone and went to him.

"What is it, Omas?" she asked in an undertone, pausing in front of him, and gazing up into the grim, painted countenance.

The Delaware returned the look for a few seconds, as if studying how to say what was in his mind. Then in a voice lower even than hers, he said—"You—little girl—big boy—go way soon—must not stay here."

"Why do you say that, Omas?"

"Iroquois like leaves on trees—white men, call Tories—soon come down here—kill all white people—kill you—kill little girl, big boy—if you stay here."

The pioneer's wife had heard the same rumors for days past. She knew there was cause for fear, for nearly all the able bodied men in Wyoming were absent with the patriot army, fighting for independence. The inhabitants in the valley had begged Congress to send some soldiers to protect them, and the relatives of the women and children had asked again and again that they might go home to save their loved ones from the Tories and Indians; but the prayer was refused. The soldiers in the army were too few to be spared, and no one away from Wyoming believed the danger as great as it was.

But the people themselves knew the peril, and did their best to prepare for it. But who should know more about the Indians and Tories than Omas, the great Delaware warrior?

When, therefore, he said these words to Mrs. Ripley, that woman's heart beat faster. She heard the laughter and prattle of the children in the house, and she thought of that bright boy, playing with his young friends not far away.

"Where can we go?" she asked, in the same guarded voice.

"With Omas," was the prompt reply; "hide in wigwam of Omas. Nobody hurt palefaced friend of Omas."

It was a trying situation. The brave woman, who had passed through many dangers with her husband, knew what a visit from the Tories and Indians meant; but she shrank from leaving Wyoming, and all her friends and neighbors.

"When will they come?" she asked; "will it be in a few weeks or in a few days?"

"Getting ready now; Brandt with Iroquois—Butler with Tory—soon be here."

"But do you mean that we shall all go with you tonight?"

The Delaware was silent for a few seconds. His active brain was busy, reviewing the situation.

"No," he finally said; "stay here till Omas come back; then go with him—all go—den no one be hurt."

"Very well; we will wait till you come to us again. We will take good care of Linna."

And without another word the Delaware turned once more, strode to the forest, which was then in fullest leaf, and vanished among the trees.

Mrs. Ripley walked slowly back to the door. On the threshold she halted, and looked around again for her absent boy. It was growing dark, and she began to feel a vague alarm for him.

A whistle fell on her ear. It was the sweetest music she had ever heard, for it came from the lips of her boy.

He was in sight, coming along the well worn path that led in front of the other dwellings and to her own door. When he saw her, he waved his hand in salutation, but could not afford to break in on the vigorous melody which kept his lips puckered.

She saw he was carrying something on his shoulder. A second glance showed that it was one of the heavy rifles used by the pioneers a hundred years ago. The sight—taken with what Omas had just said—filled her heart with forebodings.

She waited until the lad came up. He kissed her affectionately, and then in the offhand manner of a big boy, let the butt of the gun drop on the ground, leaned the top away from him, and glancing from it to his mother, asked—"What do you think of it?"

"It seems to be a good gun. Whose is it?"

"Mine," was the proud response. "Colonel Butler ordered that it be given to me, and I'm to use it, too, mother."

"For what purpose?"

"The other Colonel Butler—you know he is a cousin to ours—has got a whole lot of Tories" (who, you know, were Americans fighting against their countrymen) "and Indians, and they're coming down to wipe out Wyoming; but I guess they will find it a harder job than they think."

And to show his contempt for the danger, the muscular lad lifted his weighty weapon to a level, and pretended to sight it at a tree.

"I wish that was a Tory or one of those Six Nation Indians—wouldn't I drop him!"

The mother could not share the buoyancy of her son. She stepped outside, so as to be beyond the hearing of the little ones.

"Omas has been here; that is his little girl that you hear laughing with Alice. He has told me the same as you—the Tories and Indians are coming, and he wants us to flee with him."

"What does he mean by that?" asked the half indignant boy.

"He says they will put us all to death, and if we do not go with him, we will be killed too."

The handsome face of Benjamin Ripley took on an expression of scorn, and as he straightened up, he seemed to become several inches taller.

"He forgets that I am with you! Omas is very kind; but he and his Tory friends had better look out for themselves. Why, with the men at the fort, Colonel Butler will have several hundred."

"But they are mostly old men and boys."

"Well," said the high spirited lad, with a twinkle of his fine hazel eyes, "add up a lot of old men and boys, and the average is the same number of middle aged men, isn't it? Don't you worry, mother—things are all right. If Omas comes back, give him our thanks, and tell him we are not going to sneak off when we are needed at home."

It was hard to resist the contagion of Ben's hopefulness. The mother not only loved but respected him as much as she could have done had he been several years older. He had been her mainstay for the two years past, during which the father was absent with the patriot army; and she came to lean upon him more and more, though her heart sank when Ben began to talk of following his father into the ranks, to help in the struggle for independence.

She found herself looking upon the situation as Ben did. If so great danger threatened Wyoming, it would be cowardly for them to leave their friends to their fate. It was clear all could not find safety by going, and she would feel she was doing wrong if she gave no heed to the others.

Ben was tall and strong for his years, and the fact that he had taken the gun from Colonel Butler to be used in taking care of the settlement bound the youth in honor to do so.

"It shall be as you say," said the mother; "I cannot be as hopeful as you, but it is our duty to stay. We will not talk about it before the children."

"I want to see how a little Indian girl looks," muttered Ben with a laugh, following his mother into the house.

Alice caught sight of him, and was in his arms the next instant, while Linna rose to her feet, and stood with her forefinger between her teeth, shyly studying the newcomer.

"Helloa, Linna! how are you?" he called, setting down his young sister and catching up the little Indian. Not only that, but he gave her a resounding smack on her dusky cheek.

"I always like pretty little girls, and I'm going to be your beau: what do you say? Is it a bargain?"

It is not to be supposed that the Delaware miss caught the whole meaning of this momentous question. She was a little overwhelmed by the rush of the big boy's manner, and nodded her head about a dozen times.

"There, Alice; do you understand that?" he asked, making the room ring with his merry laughter; "I'm to be Linna's beau. How do you like it?"

"I'm glad for you, but I—guess—I oughter be sorry for Linna."

CHAPTER THREE: JULY THIRD, 1778

While Ben Ripley was frolicking with little Alice and her Indian friend Linna, the mother prepared the evening meal.

The candles were lighted, and they took their places at the table.

All this was new and strange to Linna. In her own home, she was accustomed to sit on the ground, and use only her fingers for knife and fork when taking food; but she was observant and quick, and knowing how it had been with her, her friends soon did away with her embarrassment. The mother cut her meat into small pieces, spread butter—which the visitor looked at askance—on the brown bread, and she had but to do as the rest, and all went well.

A few minutes after supper both girls became drowsy, and Mrs. Ripley, candle in hand, conducted them upstairs to the small room set apart for their use.

This was another novel experience for the visitor. She insisted at first upon lying on the hard floor, for never in her life had she touched a bed; but after awhile, she became willing to share the couch with her playmate.

Alice knelt down by the side of the little trundle bed and said her prayers, as she always did; but Linna could not understand what it meant. She wonderingly watched her until she was through, and then with some misgiving, clambered among the clothes, and the mother tucked her up, though the night was so warm they needed little covering.

Mrs. Ripley felt that she ought to tell the dusky child about her heavenly Father, and to teach her to pray. She therefore sat down on the edge of the bed, and in simple words began the wonderful story of the Saviour, who gave His life to save her as well as all others.

Alice dropped asleep right away, but Linna lay motionless, with her round black eyes fixed on the face of the lady, drinking in every word she said. By and by, however, the eyelids began to droop, and the good woman ceased. Who shall tell what precious seed was thus sown in that cabin in Wyoming, more than a hundred years ago?

While Mrs. Ripley was talking upstairs, she heard voices below; so that she knew Ben had a visitor. As she descended, she recognized a neighbor who lived on the other side of the river.

"I called," said he, "to tell you that you must lose no time in moving into Forty Fort with your little girl."

"You do not mean right away?"

"Not tonight, but the first thing in the morning."

"Is the danger so close as that?"

"Our scouts report the Tory Colonel Butler with a large force of whites and Indians marching down the valley."

"But do you not expect to repel them?"

"We are sure of that," was the confident reply; "but it won't do for any of the women and children to be exposed. The Indians will scatter, and cut off all they can. Others of our friends are out warning the people, and we must have them all in a safe place."

"Will you wait for your enemies to attack the fort?"

"I believe our Colonel Butler favors that; but others, and among them myself and Ben, favor marching out and meeting them."

"That's it," added the lad, shaking his head. "I believe in showing them we are not scared. Colonel Butler got leave of absence to come to Wyoming; he has some regulars with him, and with all our men and boys we'll teach the other Colonel Butler a lesson he won't forget as long as he lives."

"Well, if you think it best, we will move into the fort with the other people until the danger is past."

"Yes, mother; I will fight better knowing that you and Alice are safe. There's Linna! What about her?"

"Who's Linna?" asked the visitor.

"She is the little child of Omas, the Delaware warrior. He brought her here this afternoon to make Alice a visit, and promised to call tomorrow for her. Will it be safe to wait until he comes?"

The neighbor shook his head.

"You mustn't take any chances. Why don't you turn her loose to take care of herself? She can do it."

"I couldn't," the mother hastened to say; "Omas left her in our care, and I must not neglect her. She will go with us."

"I don't think it will be safe for her father to come after her, when the flurry is over."

"Why not?"

"He will be with the Iroquois, even though his tribe doesn't like them any too well; for the Iroquois are the conquerors of the Delawares, and drove them off their hunting grounds."

"Well," said Mrs. Ripley, with a sigh; "even if he never comes for her, she will always have a home with us."

The dwelling of the Ripleys was on the eastern shore of the Susquehanna. On the other side stood Fort Wintermoot and Forty Fort, the former being at the upper end of the valley. That would be the first one reached by the invaders, and the expectation was that it would give up whenever ordered to do so, for nearly all in it were friends of the Tories.

It was evident that when Omas left his child with her friends, and spoke of returning the next day, or soon thereafter, he did not know how near the invasion was. Mrs. Ripley expected that when he did learn it, he would hasten back for her.

The night, however, passed without his appearance, and the hot July sun came up over the forests on the eastern bank of the river, and still he remained away. It looked as if he had decided to let her take her chances while he joined the invaders in their work of destruction and woe.

Mrs. Ripley would have been willing to wait longer, but she was urged not to lose another hour. The frightened settlers were not allowed to take anything but their actual necessaries with them, for the cramped quarters in Forty Fort, where a number of cabins were erected, would be crowded to the utmost to make room for the hundreds who might clamor for admission. The quarters, indeed, were so scant that many camped outside, holding themselves ready to rush within should it become necessary.

Little Linna was filled with wonder when she saw her friends preparing to move and knew she was going with them. But she helped in her way as much as she could and asked no questions. There was no need, in fact, for Alice asked enough for both.

And just here I must relate to you a little history.

On the last days of June, 1778, Colonel John Butler, with about four hundred soldiers—partly made up of Tories—and six or seven hundred Indians, entered the head of Wyoming Valley. As I have said, he was a cousin of Colonel Zebulon Butler, who commanded the patriots and did all he could to check the invaders. Reaching Fort Wintermoot, the British officer sent in a demand for its surrender. The submission was made, and the invaders then came down the valley and ordered the Connecticut people to surrender Forty Fort and the settlements. Colonel Zebulon Butler had under him, to quote the historical account, "two hundred and thirty enrolled men, and seventy old people, boys, civil magistrates, and other volunteers." They formed six companies, which were mustered at Forty Fort, where the families of the settlers on the east side of the river had taken refuge.

Colonel Zebulon Butler, upon receiving the summons, called a council of war. This was on the 3rd of July. The officers believed that a little delay would be best, in the hope of the arrival of reinforcements; but nearly all the men were so clamorous to march out and give the invaders battle, that it was decided to do so.

"You are going into great danger," remarked the leader, as he mounted his horse and placed himself at the head of the patriots, "but I will go as far as any of you."

At three o'clock in the afternoon the column, numbering about three hundred, marched from the fort with drums beating and colors flying. They moved up the valley, with the river on the right and a marsh on the left, until they arrived at Fort Wintermoot, which had been set on fire by the enemy to give the impression they were withdrawing from the neighborhood.

As you may well believe, the movements of the patriots were watched with deep interest by those left behind. The women and children clustered along the river bank and strained their eyes in the direction of Fort Wintermoot, the black smoke from which rolled down the valley and helped to shut out their view.

There was hardly one among the spectators that had not a loved relative with the defenders. It might be a tottering grandfather, a sturdy son, who, though a boy, was inspired with the deepest fervor, and eager to risk his life for the sake of his mother or sister, whose hearts almost stopped beating in the painful suspense which must continue until the battle was decided.

Alice was too young fully to understand the peril in which Ben was placed. She had kissed him goodbye when he ran to take his place with the others, and, with a light jest on his lips about her and Linna, he had snatched a kiss from the little Delaware's swarthy cheek.

The mother added a few cheering words to the children, and it was a striking sight when they and a number of others, about their age or under, began playing with all the merriment of children who never dream that the world contains such afflictions as sorrow, woe, and death.

It was easy to follow the course of the patriots for a time after they were beyond sight, by the sound of their drums and the shrill whistling of several fifes.

In those days it was much more common than now for people to drink intoxicating liquors. Just before the patriots started up the valley, I am sorry to say, a few of the men drank more than they should. It has been claimed by some that but for this things would have gone differently on that day, which will live for ever as one of the saddest in American history.

By and by the anxious people near the fort noticed that the sound of drums and fifes had ceased, and the reports of firearms were heard.

They knew from this that the opposing forces were making ready for the conflict, and the suspense became painful indeed.

Then amid the rattle of musketry sounded the whoops of the Iroquois. The battle was on. Fighting began about four o'clock in the afternoon. Colonel Zebulon Butler ordered his men to fire, and at each discharge to advance a step. The fire was regular and steady, and the Americans continued to gain ground, having the advantage where it was open. Despite the exertions of the invaders, their line gave way, and but for the help of the Indians they would have been routed.

The flanking party of red men kept up a galling fire on the right, and the patriots dropped fast. The Indians on the Tory left were divided into six bands who kept up a continuous yelling which did much to inspirit each other, while the deadly aim told sadly upon the Americans.

The most powerful body of Indians was in a swamp on the left of the patriots, and by and by they outflanked them. The Americans tried to manoeuvre so as to face the new danger, but some of them mistook the order for one to retreat. Everything was thrown into confusion.

Colonel Zebulon Butler, seeing how things were going, galloped up and down between the opposing lines, calling out—"Don't leave me, my children. Stand by me and the victory is ours!"

But it was too late. The patriots could not be rallied. They were far outnumbered, and once thrown into a panic, with the captain of every company slain, the day was lost.

You cannot picture the distress of the women, children, and feeble old men waiting at Forty Fort the issue of the battle.

The sorrowful groups on the bank of the river listened to the sounds of conflict, and read the meaning as they came to their ears.

The steady, regular firing raised their hopes at first. They knew their sons and friends were fighting well, despite the shouts of the Indians borne down the valley on the sultry afternoon.

By and by the firing grew more scattering, and instead of being so far up the river as at first, it was coming closer.

This could mean but one thing; the patriots were retreating before the Tories and Indians.

One old man, nearly four score years of age, who pleaded to go into the battle, but was too feeble, could not restrain his feelings. He walked back and forth, inspired with new strength and full of hope, until the scattered firing and its approach left no doubt of its meaning.

He paused in his nervous, hobbling pace, and said to the white faced women standing breathlessly near—"Our boys are retreating: they have been beaten—all hope is gone!"

The next moment two horsemen galloped into sight. "Colonel Butler and Colonel Denison!" said the old man, recognizing them; "they bring sad news."

It was true. They rode their horses on a dead run, and reining up at the fort, where the people crowded around them, they leaped to the ground, and Colonel Butler said—"Our boys have been driven from the field, and the Tories and Indians are at their heels!"

CHAPTER FOUR: THE EASTERN SHORE

Young Ben Ripley made a good record on that eventful 3rd of July. He loaded and fired as steadily as a veteran. The smoke of the guns, the wild whooping of the Iroquois Indians, the sight of his friends and neighbors continually dropping to the ground, some of them at his elbow, the deafening discharge of the rifles—all these and the dreadful swirl and rush of events dazed him at times; but he kept at it with a steadiness which caused more than one expression of praise from the officers nearest him.

All at once he found himself mixed up in the confusion caused by the attempt to wheel a part of the line to face the flanking assailants, and the mistake of many that it was an order to retreat.

He did not know what it meant, for it seemed to him that a dozen officers were shouting conflicting orders at the same moment. A number of men threw down their guns and made a wild rush to get away, several falling over each other in the frantic scramble; others bumped together, and above the din of the conflict sounded the voices of Colonel Butler, as he rode back and forth through the smoke, begging his troops not to leave him, and victory would be theirs.

Seeing the hopeless tangle, the Indians swarmed out of the swamp, and by their savage attack and renewed shouts made the hubbub and confusion tenfold worse.

Somebody ran so violently against Ben that he was thrown to the ground. He was on his feet in an instant and turned to see who did it. It was a soldier fleeing for life from an Iroquois warrior.

Ben raised his gun, took quick aim and pulled the trigger, but no report followed. He had forgotten his weapon was unloaded.

Other forms obtruded between him and the couple, and he could not see the result of the pursuit and attack. Despite all he could do, he was forced back by the panic stricken rush around and against him.

Suddenly a wild cry reached him. An Iroquois with painted face rushed upon him with uplifted tomahawk, but he was yet several paces away, when another warrior seized his arm and wrenched him to one side.

"Run—go fast—don't stay!" commanded the Indian that had saved the youth, furiously motioning to him.

"If my gun were loaded," replied Ben, though his voice was unheard in the din, "I wouldn't go till I did something more. Helloa! is that you, Omas?"

It was the Delaware that had turned the assault aside.

A couple of bounds placed him beside he lad, and he caught his arm with a grip of iron.

It was of no use trying to hold back. Omas half running, half leaping, drove his way like a wedge through the surging swarm. His left hand closed around the upper arm of Ben, while his right grasped his tomahawk, he having thrown aside his rifle.

The boy was repeatedly jerked almost off his feet. He could run fast, but was not equal to this warrior, who forged along with resistless might. Twice did an Iroquois make for the young prisoner, as he supposed the lad to be, but a warning motion of the tomahawk upheld by Omas repelled him.

The Delaware was prudent, and instead of keeping in the midst of the surging mass, worked to one side, so that they were soon comparatively free from the tumultuous throng.

There was no attempt at conversation between the Delaware and Ben. The boy knew what was meant by this rough kindness. The day was lost, and his thoughts went out to the loved ones waiting down the valley to learn the result of the battle. He wanted to get to them as quickly as he could.

The rush carried them beyond the main body of fugitives, though not out of danger, for the Iroquois were pursuing hard; but soon Omas loosened his grip and dropped the arm of the lad. They were far enough removed from the swirl to exchange words.

"Where moder—where Alice?", asked the Delaware, as if he had no concern for his own child.

"At Forty Fort."

"Linna with them?"

"Yes; they are together with the other folks."

"Go dere—tell cross riber—make haste to Del'mware."

This command meant that the little party should hurry to the eastern side of the Susquehanna, and start for the settlements on the Upper Delaware. The nearest town was Stroudsburg, sixty miles distant, and the way led through a dismal forest.

The words of Omas showed, too, that he knew what was coming. Though the British Colonel

Butler might accept the surrender and strive to give fair treatment to the prisoners, he would find it hard to restrain the Tories and Indians.

All that could be done was for the fugitives to flee, without an hour's delay. They were already flocking to the river in the effort to reach the other side. A good many hid among the grass and undergrowth on Monacacy Island, where the Tories and Indians followed, and hunted them out without mercy.

Those who were wise enough to set out in time had a chance of arriving at the settlements on the Upper Delaware, though much suffering was sure to follow, since there was no time to prepare food to take with them.

The remark of Omas prompted Ben's words—"How can I get mother, and Alice and Linna, to the other side? They cannot swim the river."

"Linna swim," was the somewhat proud answer; "she take care of Alice you take care of moder."

"I might at any other time, but with the people crowding around us, and the Indians at our heels and shooting down all they can, what chance have we? Why can't you come with me and help them?"

No doubt the Delaware had asked himself the question, for he answered it not by words, but by breaking into a loping trot for Forty Fort, with Ben running at his side. He halted before reaching the refuge, and turned aside among the bushes overhanging the edge of the river, his actions showing he was searching for something.

He speedily found a canoe, probably his own. It had been so skillfully hidden among the dense undergrowth that one might have passed within a couple of paces without seeing it.

He picked it up as if it were a toy boat and set it down in the water.

"Go bring moder—bring Alice—bring Linna."

Ben was off like a shot, for he knew there was not a minute to throw away. It was the season when the days were longest, and two or three hours must pass before it would be fully night.

It would not do for Omas to go with Ben. His appearance at the fort would add to the panic, and be almost certain to bring about a conflict with some of the whites. It was his province to guard the precious canoe from being taken by other fugitives.

Ben Ripley now thought only of his loved ones. He knew the anguish his mother would suffer until she learned he was safe, and he forced his way to the spot where he had parted from her.

It was a sad experience. Old men, women and children, with white faces, were rushing to and fro, wringing their hands and wailing, searching for those whom they never again would see in this life; crowding into the little fort, as if they knew a minute's delay would be fatal; some making for the river, into which they plunged in a wild effort to reach the eastern shore, while among the frantic masses appeared here and there a fugitive from the scene of battle, perhaps wounded and telling his dreadful story of the defeat, with all the woeful consequences that were certain to follow.

With much difficulty and some rough work the lad reached the spot where he had bidden his mother and the children goodbye, but none of the three was in sight. They had been swept aside by the rush of the terrified people.

A cry sounded above the tumult, and before he could learn where it came from, the arms of his mother were about his neck.

"Thank Heaven! my boy is safe! You do not know what I have suffered. I could learn nothing about you. Are you hurt?"

"Not a scratch—which is more than many other poor fellows can say. Where are the children?"

A tiny hand was slipped into his own, and looking down, there stood Linna, with her forefinger between her teeth, looking shyly up at him. There could be no doubt she felt fully acquainted.

Alice came forward on the other side. Neither understood the cause of the turmoil about them. They were not scared, but were awed into silence.

"I saw Omas," explained Ben to his mother; "he saved me from the fate of many others."

"Where is he?"

"A little way off, under the bank, waiting with his canoe, to take us across the river.

"He says we must hurry through the woods for the settlements on the Upper Delaware. Every hour that we stay increases our danger."

"Let me take Alice; lead the way."

Clasping tight the hand of Linna, with his mother at his heels, Ben pushed for the point where he had left the Delaware a few minutes before.

Strange that though the distance was not far, and the confusion seemed to be increasing every minute, the little party had not gone half way when they were checked by one of the men that had been in the battle. He was slightly wounded, and under the influence of liquor.

"Who's that you've got with you?" he demanded, looking down at Linna, who saw no danger in the act.

"A friend of Alice and me."

"She looks like an Injin," added the soldier, scowling threateningly at her; "if she is, I want her."

"I told you she is a friend of ours—get out of my way!"

The soldier's condition enabled Ben to tumble him over on his back by means of a vigorous shove. Before he could steady himself and get upon his feet again, the others were beyond reach.

I am sure he would not have acted that way, had he been in the possession of his senses.

When Ben parted from Omas, he was without a rifle, but on joining him again, the warrior had a fine weapon in his hand. It was not the one with which he appeared at the house. The lad might have guessed how he got it, but he did not ask any questions, nor seem to notice it.

As the party came up, Omas merely glanced at Mrs. Ripley and her child, but did not speak. As for his own little girl, he gave her no notice. Young as she was, she understood him, and did not claim any attention from him. If they had been alone, she would have been in his arms with their cheeks together.

"Go 'cross," said he, pointing toward the other shore.

"Ben has told me what you said: we are ready," replied Mrs. Ripley.

He held the canoe steady and motioned her to take her place in it. She did so, and Alice nestled at her feet, being careful not to stir, for such frail craft are easily upset.

The canoe was small, and the weight of the mother and child sank it quite low, though it would hold another adult.

"Get in," added Omas to the lad.

Ben obeyed. He knew all about such boats, and could have paddled it across had there been a paddle to use, but there was none.

When the Delaware laid his rifle inside with Ben's, it was evident he intended to swim, towing or shoving the boat.

"Come, Linna, there's just room for you," added the youth, reaching out his hand for the dusky little girl.

Instead of obeying, she looked up at her father and said something to which he made answer brusquely, as it sounded to the others.

Retreating several paces from shore, she ran nimbly to the edge of the bank, and with a leap splashed away beyond the bow of the canoe, and began swimming like a fish for the eastern shore.

It was a real treat for her, even though she did not remove any of her clothing. The weather was sultry, and the bath refreshingly cool. Not comprehending the sad scenes around her, she dived, and splashed, and frolicked, easily keeping in advance of the boat.

Truth to tell, the canoe had all it could hold, and Omas, who swam at the stern, handled it with care to prevent it overturning. The water rose almost to the gunwales, and a little jolt or carelessness would have capsized it.

The Delaware swam high out of water. He knew the boat would attract the attention of some of his own people on the bank, who, if they thought the occupants were escaping, would either pursue or fire on them.

The sight of the Indian, however, at the stern would make it appear that they were already prisoners, and the other warriors would give their attention elsewhere.

Omas kept clear of Monacacy Island, and by and by his feet touched ground. Before that, the dripping Linna had run out on land, and so the whole party safely reached the eastern shore.

CHAPTER FIVE: IN THE WOODS

You have not forgotten what I told you about the mountain range, which shuts in Wyoming Valley on the east. It is a thousand feet in height, abounding with ravines, clefts, rocks, boulders and the most rugged kind of places.

The fugitives who fled from the Susquehanna to escape the Indians had to make their way over these mountains, and then find their way through sixty miles of trackless woods to the Delaware River. A great many succeeded in doing so, but the deaths and sufferings in the vast stretch of forest gave it the dreadful name of "The Shades of Death," by which it is often referred to even to this day.

Omas swam at the rear of the small canoe, as I told you, with Mrs. Ripley and her two children seated inside and balancing themselves with great care to prevent the heavily loaded craft from sinking or overturning.

More than one Seneca or Oneida Indian, or perhaps a Tory, that had chased some terrified fugitives to the edge of the river, halted and made ready to fire upon the canoe, whose occupants were seen to be three white persons.

When they looked again, however, they observed the head and shoulders of an Indian warrior, who was plainly propelling the craft in front of him. That was enough to satisfy them.

On the way over, Linna, the little Indian girl, amused herself by diving under the canoe, sometimes appearing on one side and then on the other, sometimes in front and then at the rear. She even ventured to impose upon her father by splashing water in his painted face. She did little of that, and he paid no attention to it.

The sun had not yet set when the grim warrior and his child emerged on the eastern shore, their garments dripping, but caring nothing for that. The boat was drawn far enough up the bank to prevent its being swept away by the current, and then all stood side by side, and as if by a common impulse, looked back at the shore they had left.

The smoke from the burning Fort Wintermoot still rested on the calm surface of the river, and filtered among the green vegetation near the scene of the battle. Other buildings had been fired, and mingled their vapor with it.

Here and there, every minute or two, sounded the sharp crack of a rifle. This too often meant that some fugitive had been run down by his cruel pursuer, who listened to no pleadings for mercy. A good many had taken refuge on Monacacy Island, from which the reports of guns continually came.

I have not the space here to tell you of the wonderful escapes at Wyoming, the particulars of which I have given in another work.

One boy, who was with several men near Fort Jenkins before the battle, saw all the men shot down or captured; but he hid himself among some willows and was not noticed.

If you ever visit the scene of the battle, you will notice a broad, flat stone, called Queen Esther's Rock, a half dozen miles below Wilkesbarre. Queen Esther was an old, cruel, half breed woman who came with the Indians. She is sometimes known as Katharine Montour. A son of hers was killed in the conflict, and she was so angered that she had sixteen captives placed around the rock, and meant to slay them all, while the warriors prevented them from escaping.

Nevertheless two of the young men jumped up and started on a run for the river. The guards dashed after them. One caught his toe, and rolled headlong down the bank into some bushes. Instead of springing up again, as he first started to do, he lay still, and though the Indians almost stepped upon him, he was not discovered, and got off without harm.

The other reached the river, took a running leap and dived, and swam under water as far as he could. When he came up to breathe, the waiting red men fired at him again and again. He was wounded, but not badly, and, reaching the other side, caught a stray horse, made a bridle from a hickory withe, and soon joined his friend.

Another fugitive, after running until he was so tired out he could hardly stand, and hearing the Indians near, backed into a hollow log and awaited his fate. He had been in the hollow but a few minutes when a spider spun its web across the entrance. A few minutes later, two warriors sat down on the log. They noticed how good a hiding place it would be for the white man, and one of them leaned over to peep in. As he did so, he saw the spider web. He was sure that it would not be there if the man was inside, and did not search further. When the warriors left, the man crawled out and got safely away.

You know that the home of the Ripleys was on the eastern shore, which they left that same morning. They had crossed over in a large flatboat with a number of other families, so that now they were near their own home again. Omas had guided the canoe, too, so they landed not far from the little structure.

"Omas," said the mother, "I understand you wish us to go to the Delaware."

"Yes," he replied, "Iroquois won't hurt you there—must go."

"We haven't a particle of food with us; Ben has his gun and may have a chance to shoot some game on the way—more than likely, he will have no chance at all; it will take us several days to reach Stroudsburg, which, I believe, is the nearest point. Don't you think it best that we should stop at the house and get what food we can?"

"Yes, we do dat; come 'long; not great time."

There could be no safer guide than the Delaware, when his race were such complete masters of the situation; though there was risk that a patriot hiding somewhere in the neighborhood might take a shot at him, under the belief that he meant harm to the captives.

The humble log structure was found just as it was left that morning. If any of the marauding bands of Indians paid it a visit, they did not linger after seeing it was tenantless.

There was a whole loaf of bread and part of another left beside some cooked chicken, and a number of live ones were scratching the ground outside, as if they had no concern in what was going on.

"The weather is warm now," remarked the prudent housewife, "but a cold storm may set in before we reach shelter."

With which she folded a blanket from her bed and laid it over her arm.

"It will come handy to sleep on," added Ben, who did the same with a second, despite the weight of his rifle, which (as they were made in those days) was a good load of itself for a strong boy.

Omas showed some impatience, though his companions did not understand the cause. His actions, indeed, were curious. They supposed he meant to conduct them all or a greater part of the way to Stroudsburg, though at times he appeared to be hesitating over it, or over some other scheme he had in mind.

Ben Ripley had rambled among the rugged scenery, on the eastern shore of the river, having gone with his father many times when he was on hunting excursions; but he was not as familiar with the ins and outs of the mountains as the Delaware, whose village was a good many miles away.

None of the party had eaten anything of account since the early morning meal, before they crossed the Susquehanna. The dangers, excitement, and suspense of the hours drove away the thought of food. Young as was Linna, she had already learned not to ask for it when either of her parents chose not to offer it to her. Doubtless she was hungry, but if so, no one else knew it. Alice had been given bread when at Forty Fort, and she now suggested that some more would not come amiss.

"We all need it," said Ben; "why not take our last meal in our old home? You have no objection Omas?"

"Eat here," was his reply.

The guns were leaned against the walls, the blankets put aside and all gathered round the board. The Delaware had done the same before when visiting the family, and acquired the civilized form of eating, while Linna picked it up during the brief time spent with her friends.

The meal lasted but a few minutes, when they once more gathered up their luggage, as it may be called, left the house, and with Omas in the lead, struck into the mountains on the long tramp to the Delaware.

The sun went down while they were picking their way through the rough section. The Ripleys expected to do much hard travelling, but their guide's knowledge of every turn enabled him to pick out paths which none ever suspected. Sometimes the climbing was abrupt, but all, even to Alice, were accustomed to that kind of work, and they kept up a steady gait, which must have placed many miles to the rear if continued long.

Omas continued at the head. Directly behind him walked his child, the path most of the time being so narrow that they were obliged to travel in Indian file. Then came Alice and her mother, while Ben considered himself the rearguard. When the space allowed, Alice took the hand of her parent, but Linna never presumed to speak to or interfere with her grim, silent parent.

Darkness closed around them before they had gone a couple of miles. During all this time the tramp continued in silence, probably not a dozen words being spoken. Each of the three elder was using eyes and ears to the utmost.

The sharp crack of a rifle broke the silence, not more than a hundred yards to the right of them. Everyone started except Omas, who acted as if he did not hear the report. He made no change in his pace, and so far as the others could see in the gloom, did not turn his head. They concluded, therefore, that no cause for alarm existed.

Fairly through the mountain spur and among the deep woods, the journey was pushed until the night was well along. Suddenly, Omas made a short turn to the right and stopping in a hollow, where there were several large boulders, he said—"We stay here all night."

The words were a surprise, for it was expected he would travel for a long time. He, Mrs. Ripley and Linna could have done so without inconvenience, but Alice was tired out. Her relatives were pretty well burdened already, though either would have carried her had it been necessary; but the party had gained so good a start that there seemed little risk in making a long stop.

Omas reached down one hand and laid it on the bare head of Alice, saying in a voice of strange gentleness—"Little girl tired—she can rest."

And then all knew he had ceased walking because of her. Had she not been a member of the party, he would have kept the rest on their feet until the sun appeared above the forest.

"Yes, I'm tired, Omas," said the little one wearily, holding the hand of the Delaware in both her own; "I'm glad you stopped."

The gloom was so deep, for there was no moon until very late (and if there had been, its rays could not have pierced the dense foliage), that they could hardly see each other's figures. Omas hastily gathered some leaves and dead twigs, which were heaped together against one of the boulders. Then he produced his flint and steel—for he had learned the trick long before of the whites—and by and by a shower of sparks was flying from the swift, sharp blows of the metal against the hard stone. A minute later one of the sparks "caught," and under his nursing a fire was speedily under way.

While he was thus engaged, Mrs. Ripley spread the blankets on the ground and Alice stretched her tired little body upon one of them.

"Mamma, I guess God will excuse me for not saying my prayers," she murmured, as she closed her eyes and sank into slumber.

Linna was tired, too, but she kept her feet and looked at her father for his permission, before presuming to lie down.

"Come, Linna, here is your place beside Alice," said the mother kindly.

Again she turned to her father, who was standing by the fire, looking off in the gloom, as if he suspected something wrong.

He gave the permission in their native tongue and she cuddled down beside her friend without further waiting.

"Mother," said Ben, "you had better lie down with them."

"Not yet," she replied, with a significant look at he Delaware, whose back was toward them.

"What about him?" asked the surprised lad in a low voice.

"He is meditating something evil: he wants to leave us.

"What evil is there in that, if he thinks we have gone far enough to be safe?"

"You have forgotten that he fought with the Iroquois today; he wants to go back to Wyoming and join them in their work."

"If that is so, how can we hinder him?"

"I don't know that we can; but I shall try it."

Ben busied himself gathering more wood, so that the fire cast a glow several yards from where it burned against the boulder.

When he had collected enough to last a long while, he came back and sat down by his mother. All this time the Delaware remained motionless, with his face away from them. He was debating some troublous question in his mind. They watched him closely.

He turned about abruptly, and said—"Omas must go—he say 'goodnight' to his friends."

CHAPTER SIX: PUSHING EASTWARD

No person in all the world is so quick to detect deception as a mother. It is simply wonderful the way she will sometimes read one's thoughts. I am sure you boys who have lagged on the road when sent on an errand, had a scrimmage with some other boy, or done any one of the numerous acts in which a mother persists in asking annoying questions, will agree with me.

While Omas, the Delaware warrior, stood with his face turned away from the camp fire and looking off in the gloom, as if he was trying to discover something in the darkness, Mrs. Ripley was sure she knew what the trouble was: he was trying to decide whether he should stay longer with the little party or leave them to make the rest of their way through the woods without him.

He might well say they were now so far from Wyoming that they were in little danger. They had but to keep on tramping for several days and nights, and they would reach the little town of Stroudsburg, which, you may know, is near Delaware Water Gap. There they need have no fear of the red men.

Mrs. Ripley knew all this as well as Omas himself, but she did not wish him to go back and join the hostile Iroquois, as he wanted to do. She felt it would be far better if he would stay with them, for then he would do no further harm to the white people.

When, therefore, he turned about and bade them goodbye, all doubt was gone. Ben did not reply, but his mother rose from the other blanket on which she had been sitting, walked quietly to where the Delaware was standing, and laid her hand kindly on his arm.

"Omas, I do not wish you to leave us," she said.

He looked at her, for both stood where the firelight fell upon their faces, and replied—"No danger—walk towards the rising sun—need not walk fast—Iroquois won't hurt—soon be safe."

The lady was too wise to let her real objection appear.

"A while ago we heard the noise of a gun; our people are fleeing through the woods, and the red men are following them. Alice is tired, and we have stopped to rest. When we start again tomorrow, some of the red men will be ahead of us. What shall we do without our friend Omas?"

"He have gun." he replied, indicating Ben.

"So have the red men, and there are more of them."

Now, if Mrs. Ripley was skilful in reading the thoughts of the Delaware, it may be that he, too, suspected the real cause for her objections. Be that as it may, it was plain he was not satisfied. He held the Ripley family in too high regard to offend them openly; but Omas was set in his ways.

He made no reply to the last remark, but stepped a little nearer the fire and sat down, moody and silent.

"You have said enough, mother," remarked Ben in a low voice; "it will anger him to say more. I will sit with my head against the rock; do you lie down on the blanket and let your head rest in my lap. I think it will be safe for us all."

With some hesitation the mother complied, the Delaware apparently paying no heed to them. He kept his seat on the ground, looking gloomily into the fire and in deep thought. A struggle was going on in his mind, and no one could say whether the good or evil would win.

Ben Ripley was anxious that his mother should sleep. She had undergone the severest of trials since early morning, and none had wrought harder than she. The morrow would make further demands on her strength. As for himself, he was young, sturdy, and could stand more and rally sooner than she.

When, therefore, she said something in a low tone, he placed his hand softly over her mouth and whispered—"S—h! go to sleep, baby."

He smoothed the silky hair away from the forehead so gently and so soothingly that she could not resist the effect. She meant to keep awake until Omas made his final decision; but no person can resist the approach of slumber, except by active movement.

Before long, and while Ben's hand was still gliding like down over the forehead, the faint, regular breathing showed she was asleep.

The son smiled.

"Good! The best mother that ever lived! Heavenly Father, watch over her and spare her for many years. Watch over us all."

He looked across at Omas, on the other side of the camp fire, and saw the Delaware gazing fixedly at him.

He arose as silently as a shadow and stepped nearer, peering down on the pale, handsome face with its closed eyes.

"She sleep?" asked the Indian.

"Yes," replied Ben, softly, with a nod of his head.

He looked at her a moment and then across to the other blanket, where the round, chubby cheeks of the little girls reflected the firelight. He waited a moment, and then the gentler side of his nature triumphed. He bent over the forms, kissed each in turn, straightened up, and pointing to the eastward, said to Ben—"Go dat way—you safe—goodbye."

"Goodbye," replied the lad, knowing it was useless to protest.

Like the gliding of the shadow of a cloud, the Delaware passed beyond the circle of light thrown out by the fire into the deep gloom of the wood. The moccasins pressed the dry leaves without giving back any sound, and he vanished.

"That makes a change of situation," was the conclusion of Ben Ripley; "he's gone, and I become the general of this army; there's no telling what danger may be abroad tonight, so I will keep my eyes open till sunrise, to make sure that no harm comes to these folks."

And ten minutes after this decision the lad was as sound asleep as his mother and the two little ones.

But there was One who did not slumber while all were unconscious. He ever watches over His children, and,—though there were many perils abroad that night, none of them came near our friends.

The camp fire which had been burning so brightly grew dimmer and lower until the figures could hardly be seen. They gradually became more indistinct, and finally the gloom was as deep as anywhere in the dense woods. Only a few smouldering embers were left, and they gave out no glow.

Ben was still sleeping, when something tickled his nose. He rubbed it vigorously with his forefinger and opened his eyes, confused and bewildered.

An odd, chuckling laugh at his elbow drew his gaze hither. There stood Linna, with the sprig of oak which she had been passing back and forth under the base of his nose, making it feel for all the world like a fly titillating his nostrils.

Ben made an attempt to catch the mischievous girl, but she deftly eluded him, and laughed so heartily that the others awoke and looked wonderingly to learn what it all meant.

"I'll pay you for that!" exclaimed the lad, as his mother raised her head from his lap. Bounding to his feet, he darted after Linna, but she was so nimble, and dodged back and forth and from right to left so fast, that it took much effort to run her down.

Like all little girls, she was very "ticklish," and when he dallied with his fingers about her plump neck, she dropped to the ground and kicked and rolled over to get away from him. He let her up, and said with pretended gravity that he never allowed any trifling with him without punishing the person therefore.

Linna did not seem to notice the absence of her father, and asked no questions. Ben told his mother how he went off after she fell asleep, and the good woman saddened, for she was sure she understood it all.

The first thing done, after a few minutes' talk, was to kneel in prayer, Mrs. Ripley leading in a petition to Heaven that all might be preserved from harm and reach the distant settlement safely. She did not forget the absent Omas, or the hundreds of hapless people whom they had left behind, who were still in great danger.

It was Mrs. Ripley's custom always to offer prayer in the little household at the beginning of each day. Linna, who had gained a dim idea of what the touching act meant, bent on her knees beside Alice; and who shall say the petition which went up from her heart was not heard and remembered by Him who notices the fall of every sparrow.

And now came the serious business of the day. Many long miles of trackless forest lay before them and the delay caused all to feel the need of hurry.

Mrs. Ripley gave to each a moderate portion of the food brought with them, carefully preserving what was left, for they were sure to need that and much more before reaching the end of their journey. The day promised to be sultry like the preceding one, and each sadly missed the water with which to quench their thirst and splash upon their faces and hands.

"We shall come across some before long," said Ben hopefully when he and his mother had divided the luggage between them and set out toward the rising sun; "we are a great deal better off than the poor folks of Wyoming."

The mother pinched the clothing of Linna, and found it dried of the moisture gained by her swim in the Susquehanna.

It is a curious practice among not only the Indians, but with many white people, not to change wet stockings or garments for dry ones. I knew a fisherman's boy whose father once punished him for removing his saturated stockings and shoes for others.

"Always let 'em dry on you, and you won't catch cold," was his doctrine. "Keep moving if you can, but don't change 'em."

I don't believe in the practice; but be that as it may, the little Delaware girl showed no ill effects from sleeping in the clothing that had been wet. As for her father, he would have been insulted at the mention of such a thing to him.

Ben's belief about finding water proved true. They had gone hardly a half mile from camp when they came upon a sparkling brook, cold and clear, and abundant enough to serve all. Having no vessels with them, they lay down and quaffed their fill. Then they bathed their faces and hands in the delicious fluid, and were much refreshed.

The expectation was that they would travel a good many miles before night again overtook them. The way, while rough and broken in many places, was not hard, and all, even to the smaller children, were used to being on their feet. There was little fear indeed that Linna would not do her part as well as the older ones. Young as she was in years, she had been trained to hardship from the time she could walk. Not only that, but, like all her race, she had learned to bear suffering in silence and without sign of pain.

She would have to become very tired before her companions would know it.

By and by the ground was found to be rising, and in the course of an hour they gained an elevation which, having few trees, gave them an extended view of the surrounding country.

Looking back in the direction of Wyoming, the sky was seen to be soiled by the heavy smoke not only from the burned Fort Wintermoot, but from other buildings that had been fired by the Tories and Indians. The sight was a sorrowful one, and caused the mother and son some uneasiness. They seemed nearer to the scene of the conflict than they had supposed, and—since the people had been continually swimming the river, and taking flight in the woods for the same point that was the destination of the Ripleys—it was quite certain that some of the pursuers were not far off.

"We must make as little noise as we can," said Ben, when the party were about to start forward again: "for there can be no telling how close we are to Indians that are looking for us.'

"I think it better for you to walk a little way in front," suggested the mother, "so as to warn us in time."

"The plan is a good one. I will keep in sight of you, and the minute I see anything amiss, will make a sign, so you can stop at once."

This course was adopted. Ben carried one of the blankets flung over his left arm as if it were an extra garment, and steadied the heavy rifle on his shoulder with the other. As you remember, he was tall for his years, strong, and with rugged health.

Had the weather been cooler he could have Kept up this method of traveling for hours without fatigue; but the heat made it trying. True, at that season of the year the foliage was dense on the trees and shut out the sun's rays, except in the open spaces and natural clearings which they now and then crossed; but the vegetation also stopped whatever breeze was stirring, and obliged the members of the party to halt many times to rest and cool themselves.

Mrs. Ripley had but few extra things to carry, and showed less fatigue than anyone, excepting the Delaware child. The latter and Alice walked most of the time side by side, and generally with clasped hands. There was no use of their trying to keep their tongues still, but they were wise enough to speak in whispers and such soft undertones that no one else could tell what they said, and therefore nothing was to be feared on that account from any enemies in the neighborhood.

"Why not he make sign?" was the startling question of Linna, pointing at Ben, before the party had gone far after their brief rest.

"What do you mean?" asked the puzzled Mrs. Ripley; "he isn't to make any sign to us till he sees or hears something wrong."

"People off dere!" replied Linna, pointing ahead and to the right of their course. "Me hear dem speak."

It was true. The keen ears of the child had discovered a peril that no one else suspected. She alone had caught the sound of voices that escaped all other ears.

CHAPTER SEVEN: JABEZ ZITNER

At this moment Ben Ripley was about a hundred feet in advance of the party and ascending a ridge in the woods, which were so open that he was in plain sight of the others.

Mrs. Ripley, on hearing the alarming words of the little Delaware girl, came to a stop. It seemed strange that Linna should have caught the sounds noticed by no one else, and that, too, while she was whispering to her companion, Alice; but even at that tender age the inherited sharpness of hearing had been trained to a wonderfully fine degree.

Mrs. Ripley was too prudent to argue with her. It was not wise to take any chances. Above all, it was important that Ben should know the truth, for he was still walking away from them with no knowledge of their discovery.

"S—h!" The sibilant noise made by the mother's lips crossed the space and the listening lad halted and looked round. She did not speak, but beckoned him to come back. He obeyed at once.

"Linna says she heard voices a minute ago, over yonder," whispered Mrs. Ripley, as her son joined them.

"So me did," added Linna, in answer to the inquiring look of the lad.

"You have sharp ears, little one; but are you sure?"

"Me am," was the confident reply.

"Where were they?"

She again pointed out the direction.

"That must be looked into: wait till I come back, and—"

"S—h!" interrupted the mother.

All caught an indistinct murmur, which proved Linna was right.

"Me tell you—eh?" she said in a proud undertone, her black eyes sparkling with triumph.

"You are right: wait till I learn whether they are friends or enemies. I will not be gone long."

Leaving the anxious group clustered together, Ben faced in the direction of the sounds, which had stopped, and were so faint when heard that he could not tell whether they belonged to friends or foes.

As nearly as he could find out, the parties were just beyond the crest of the ridge, and, but for the warning of Linna, he would have run into the danger before knowing it.

With the utmost care he went up the slope. He leaned forward and stepped more slowly, avoiding, so far as he could, making any noise on the leaves or against the bushes and limbs which he had to push aside to allow him to advance.

At the instant of reaching the highest point he heard the voices again, so close that he knew they were made by white people, who were in a clump of dense undergrowth. A faint wreath of smoke filtering through the branches overhead showed they had started a small fire, beside which they were probably sitting or reclining on the ground.

Now that he was certain they belonged to his own race, he had less fear. Still, they might prove unpleasant neighbors when they came to know one of the party was a daughter of Omas. Turning toward his friends, who were watching him, Ben made a sign for them to stay where they were while he went forward.

He moved with the same care as before, but an unexpected accident spoiled everything. His foot caught in a wire-like vine, and he almost fell on his hands and knees. Aware that he had betrayed himself, he threw aside further caution, hurried down the slope, and called out in a guarded undertone—

"Helloa there, friends!"

"Who are you?" was the demand that instantly followed, and from the undergrowth, beside a small fire, two men suddenly rose upright, each with rifle in hand.

Ben recognized them. One was Jabez Zitner and the other Horace Burwink—both middle aged, sturdy, and strong. They were neighbors, and had taken part in the engagement the day before, but, escaping without harm, were now on their way to the settlements of the Upper Delaware.

A meeting of this kind would have been pleasing in the highest degree, for it added great strength to the party; but a misgiving came to the lad when he recognized Zitner. He was the man who, when partially intoxicated the previous afternoon, had tried to take Linna from him and was vigorously shoved aside by her friend.

"Helloa, Ben! where did you come from?" asked Zitner, who was now entirely himself.

"Glad to see you," added Burwink, and the two extended their hands. "You gave us a great scare, for the woods are full of redskins."

"You startled me, too," replied Ben. "I am travelling with my mother and sister to Stroudsburg. I suppose you are aiming for the same place?"

"Yes—if we ever get there. What become of that little sarpent you had with you yesterday?"

It was Zitner who asked the question. Ben's face flushed, for he did not like to hear Linna spoken of in that way.

"She is with us," he quietly replied.

"What are you going to do with her?"

"She is in our care, and goes wherever we go."

"You seem mighty fond of the people who played the mischief with us yesterday."

"Jabez Zitner, I fought just as hard as you, and did all I could to drive back the Iroquois and Tories, but I don't fight little children six years old."

"Who's talking about fighting 'em?" demanded Zitner angrily. "Their people didn't spare our women and children."

"They are savages, but you and I claim to be civilized."

"That's all well enough, but my motto is—fight fire with fire." Burwink was listening to this sharp interchange of words, the meaning of which he caught. Wishing to make a friend of him, for Ben foresaw trouble, he asked—"Am I not right, Mr. Burwink?"

"I should say—on general principles you are; but, after yesterday, I don't feel much love for any of the varmints. Who is this Injin gal that you are talking about?"

Ben was too wise to give the name of Linna's father, knowing he would be instantly recognized as one of the fiercest warriors that had taken part in the invasion and battle. He therefore replied—

"She is a girl named Linna; she is of the same age as our Alice, and was visiting her when we crossed the river to Forty Fort yesterday morning. We could do nothing but take her with us, and I will defend her with my life."

"You are talking big," remarked Zitner, with a scornful look at the sturdy lad. "Who is the gal's father?"

"That makes no difference; but I will say he belongs to the Delaware tribe, most of whom are friends to our people."

"There were plenty of them with the Senecas and Oneidas yesterday, and they fought like wild cats, too. But why don't you bring your folks forward?" added Zitner, looking inquiringly around.

"I will do so. Wait a few minutes."

He strode back and over the top of the ridge, until he caught sight of the frightened group.

"Come on!" he called, beckoning to them. "Mr. Zitner and Burwink are here, and want to see you."

With an expression of thankfulness, Mrs. Ripley, clasping a hand of each of the children, walked up the slope, and passed over to where the couple awaited their approach by the camp fire. She shook hands with each, and expressed her pleasure at meeting them. They did the same toward her, and then all, with the exception of the children, seated themselves on the fallen tree beside which the small fire was burning.

Mrs. Ripley had observed the little incident the preceding afternoon, when Zitner tried to stop Linna. She was ill at ease, for she noticed how sharply he looked at the child. She hoped, however, that now he was fully himself, he would be ashamed of his action, or at least make no reference to it.

No fear of her doing so. She showed her tact by leading the conversation in another direction.

"When did you leave Wyoming?"

"Burwink and I didn't get a chance to swim over until nearly midnight, and then we had a rough time of it. There were plenty of others that tried to do the same and never got to this side."

"When did you leave?" asked Burwink of the lady.

"We crossed before it was dark."

"How did you manage it? Swim?"

"No; we came over in a canoe. A Delaware Indian, the father of Linna, swam behind the boat and pushed it across. But for him, we never could have gotten away."

Mrs. Ripley, like her son, meant to keep the name of their friend from these men. There was no danger of either her or Ben telling it; but neither thought of another means they had of learning it.

At this point, Alice went to her mother and leaned against her knees, with her gaze on the faces of the men. She had been standing beside Linna, whose eyes were never once removed from the displeasing countenance of Zitner.

She must have noticed the incident referred to, for the expression on her round face was of dislike and distrust. She stood further off from the men than anyone else—silent, watchful, and suspicious.

Zitner now looked at her.

"Come here," he said coaxingly, extending his hand.

"No; me won't. Me don't like you," she replied, with an angry flirt and backward step.

"Jingo!" exclaimed the surprised Zitner; "I didn't think she could talk our lingo. Say, Miss Spitfire, what is your father's name?"

Before either Mrs. Ripley or her son could interpose, Linna answered defiantly—"He Omas— great warrior—kill good many white people—kill you!"

The reply caused consternation on the part of Mrs. Ripley and Ben, but the boy shut his lips tight. He could not but admire the bravery of the child, and he was determined to stand by her to the end.

The mother was in despair, but she relied mainly on persuasion and prayer.

With no idea of what all this meant, Alice looked in the face of each person in turn while speaking.

"She's a chip off the old block," said Burwink, with a laugh. "She doesn't seem to have much fear of you, Jabez."

"I am hopeful she will feel different when she grows older," soothingly remarked Mrs. Ripley.

"I'd like to know what you build your hope on," replied Zitner, still curiously watching the child.

"I expect to have her a good deal under my care, and I shall do all I can to instruct her aright. This morning she knelt with us in prayer. You must remember she is very young, and has heard little, if anything, of Christianity."

Zitner shook his head.

"It's born in 'em, and you can't get it out."

"But, Mr. Zitner, you will not deny that we have a good many Christian Indians. There are plenty of them at Gnadenhutten, and the Moravian missionaries have been the means of turning hundreds from darkness to light. If they can do that with full grown warriors and women, may we not hope for the best from those of tender years?"

"I don't know about that," was the dogged reply. "I never believed in this conversion business."

"What can you mean by such a remark?" asked the shocked lady.

"I mean, religion is good enough for white people, but don't work with Injins. They will pretend they're good, but are only waiting for a chance to do mischief."

"The converted Delawares have never taken part in the wars against us. You know that as well as I."

"How about Omas?"

"He makes no pretence of Christianity."

"And therefore has no claim on our indulgence."

"No one has said he has," observed Ben, coming to his mother's help; "he will never ask quarter from you or any white man."

"Where is he now? He brought you over the river, but seems to have deserted you."

"He left because he didn't think we had further need of his aid; we can get along without him."

"Now, see here," added Zitner, straightening up on the log and slapping his knee; "I'll tell you what I've made up my mind to do. I am willing to give in to Mrs. Ripley that far, that I won't harm that youngster—that is, I will leave it to her father whether I shall or shan't."

Neither mother nor son could understand the meaning of this strange remark. They waited for the man to explain.

"I'm going to take her with us as a hostage. We're not clear of the varmints yet. I believe Omas himself ain't far off, and the rest will be on our heels all the way to Stroudsburg. If they get us in a tight place, I'll let 'em know we've got the gal of Omas with us, and if they harm a hair of our heads it'll be all up with her. We'll take her clean to Stroudsburg, and then turn her loose, for we won't have any further need of her; but she must go with us."

"Jabez Zitner," said Ben Ripley—"the moment you lay your hand on that child I will shoot you!"

CHAPTER EIGHT: LINNA'S WOODCRAFT

No one could have looked into the face of Ben Ripley without seeing he meant just what he said.

Jabez Zitner supposed, when he made known that he intended to take the little Delaware girl with him as a hostage, that though it might be displeasing to the Ripleys, they would not dare object; but he was mistaken.

The lad was sitting furthest away on the fallen tree, with his rifle resting across his knees, when he warned the man that if he laid a hand on Linna he would shoot him.

Ben spoke low, but mingling with his words were two faint clicking sounds. They were made by the hammer of his rifle, as with his thumb he drew it back ready for use. His face was slightly pale, but his eyes glittered, and he rose to his feet and looked at the startled man.

Mrs. Ripley gave a gasp of fright and clasped her hands, while the children mutely stared.

Even Zitner was silent. He knew Ben's pluck, but did not believe it would take him thus far, for it looked as if there were two adults against a single boy.

Burwink however, was more of a man than his companion. He looked smilingly at Ben and said—"Jabez, I reckon this has gone far enough."

"What do you mean?'" angrily asked the other.

"You must leave the little gal alone."

"Oh, thank you! thank you!" exclaimed Mrs. Ripley. "I might have known you would see that right is done."

Zitner had a few sharp words with his friend, but the latter was immovable. He would not listen to his proposition, and that ended the matter.

"Well," finally said Zitner, rising to his feet, "I intended to see you folks safe to the Delaware; but I won't have anything to do with you now. Come, Horace."

He strode off without another word or looking to the right or left. Burwink waited a minute, and then, with a quizzical look at Mrs. Ripley and her son asked—

"Do you think you can stand it?"

"We shall have to," replied Ben.

"Well, goodbye, and good luck to you;" and he followed his friend among the trees.

"That was a luckier ending than I expected," remarked Ben, letting down the hammer of his rifle.

"If Mr. Burwink had sided with him, there would have been no help for it," said his mother.

"Such people are always cowards. I wasn't afraid of him."

Now that they had departed, Linna came over to her champion—though she could not have fully understood all that had passed—and placed her hand confidingly on his shoulder.

"Linna, I have two sisters," he said tenderly; "yonder is one, and her name is Alice: can you tell me the name of the other?"

"Yes—she name be Linna."

"You are right. Now, if you will kiss me, I won't tickle you any more for making my nose itch this morning."

The lips were put up to his, and with deep affection on the part of both, the salute was exchanged.

"If any more white people show themselves, and they ask you your father's name, let mother and me answer for you."

"Me do what you say," was the obedient response.

It need not be said that our friends were greatly relieved by the departure of Zitner. While as I have already said, they ought to have been glad of the company of him and Burwink, they would have been ill at ease so long as the surly fellow was with them. He surely held no good will toward the little girl, and would have found some chance to show it.

"But are we really rid of him?" asked Ben of his mother. The two sat close to each other on the tree, and the children were playing a few steps away.

"I am quite sure we are."

"He may steal back tonight, if we camp near."

"Why should he? He does not want to harm Linna, but to use her as a means of safety against her own people."

"That was what he said, but I don't believe him. It seems to me we ought to change our course, to be certain of not meeting him again."

"As you think best."

"We have had a good rest. Come, girls, we must be off." Taking the lead as before, Ben strode down the incline, bearing more to the left than he had been doing.

All smiled at Linna, for she noticed the change on the instant.

"You go wrong," she said; "dat not right way."

"Which is the right way, Miss Smartness?"

She pointed it out.

"You are right, but that is the course of that bad man, who doesn't like you. We will go around, so as not to see him again."

She was satisfied, and gave her attention to Alice, who thought it odd that she and Ben should have so many disputes.

Over the varying surface, turning aside now and then to pass some obstacle in the shape of rocks or ravines—now up hill and down, among the dense trees, where the briars and bushes scratched their hands and faces, across small rippling streams and natural clearings—they pushed on until the sun was far beyond meridian and the halt and rest were grateful.

"I don't think we need give any more thought to Zitner," said Ben; "and I am sure we are all glad. He could not find us now, if he tried."

"If they kept to their course, we must be several miles apart."

"I have been working my way back, so that, after all, I do not think we have lost much ground. I hope Miss Linna is satisfied."

"She would make complaint if she was not."

They had stopped near another of the small running streams, for it was harder to do without water than food.

"I'm hungry, mother."

"So we all are," she added, producing half a loaf, which was the last of their food.

"To leave any portion of this will only aggravate all your appetites, so we will finish it."

The bread was divided among the four, and when eating ceased not a crumb was left.

"It isn't a good time of the year for hunting, mother, but if I can get sight of any game, I'll bring it down, whether it is a deer, bear, wild turkey, quail, or anything that will serve for a meal."

"It isn't a time to be particular—in watching for danger look also for game."

"That's what I have been doing for the last few hours."

With the passage of time and the increase of the distance between them and Wyoming the hopes of the little party naturally rose. They were now a good many miles from their old home, and as yet had not seen a single red man. That numbers were abroad there could be no doubt, although it is a fact that a great many people did not start eastward until several days after the battle.

But it was a long, long way to the Delaware, with the travelling such as they had to face. I have spoken of the forest as being trackless and a wrong impression may have been given. An old trail led from the Susquehanna to the Delaware, and was followed by many of the fugitives; but great risk was run by those who did so, for most of the pursuers used the same path. As a consequence, some were overtaken and slain.

Those who avoided the beaten route of necessity suffered greater hardships; but none was equal to that of meeting their enemies. Omas took care to steer wide of this trail when leading the party into the wild section to the east of the river, and he showed them that he wished them to do the same. Ben was too wise to forget his wishes.

The location of the sun in the sky, the appearance of the bark and moss, and the tops of certain trees, enabled the young woodman to keep a pretty true course. He remarked, with a laugh, that if there was any likelihood of going wrong, Linna would correct him.

The afternoon was well past before they came upon any more water, and, with the warm weather and their long tramp, all suffered from thirst. They were not traversing a desert country, however, and soon found what they wanted in abundance.

"But," said Ben, "I am worried about food, mother. It is nearly night, and we haven't a mouthful. I suppose if there was plenty, I wouldn't feel half as bad, but it seems to me I was never so hungry in all my life."

"That is natural; but, if necessary, we can go all night without food."

"If necessary, of course we can, but I dread it. Alice and Linna will suffer, though I'm not so sure about Linna. I would give almost anything for a wild turkey."

The dusky child looked up from where she was sitting on the ground, playing with Alice.

"Want turkey—eh?" she asked.

"Yes; have you any to sell?"

"Me get you one."

Mother and son stared in amazement. They could not believe she was in earnest. She saw it and, with a grin, added—"Omas showed Linna how get turkey."

"What can she be driving at?" asked the puzzled Ben. "She surely would not say what she does without reason. Linna, teach Ben how to get a wild turkey; we want one for supper, for if we don't have it, we shall all have to go without food."

"Me hungry," she ventured; "so be Alice—so be you."

"You are right. Come, sister, show me how to catch a turkey."

She gravely rose from the ground. Her face appeared serious, but those who looked at her closely detected a sparkle of the black eyes, for all the world as if she meditated some prank upon her confiding friends. Ben was suspicious. She added—

"Go wid me—me show you." Then he was sure she was up to something.

He rose from where he was sitting, and, rifle in hand, walked a little way in the wood. She looked round once or twice, and continued advancing a few minutes after they were out of sight of Alice and her mother.

She held the hand of the youth, who acted as if he was a bad boy being led to punishment. He started to ask a question, but she checked him by raising her forefinger and a "S—h!" and he did not presume again.

Finally she stopped among a number of trees where several trunks were two or three feet in diameter. Stepping behind one, she motioned him to do the same with another a few yards off. Surveying him a moment, as if to make sure he was doing right, she suddenly emitted a sound from between her lips, which caused Ben Ripley to utter the exclamation under his breath— "Well, by gracious! If that doesn't beat everything!"

"Why don't shoot?" she abruptly asked.

The call made by Linna was the exact imitation of a wild turkey when lost in the woods. Perhaps you may know that the body of every one of those birds contains a bone which a hunter can so use as to make the same signal; but it is hard to produce the sound without such help, though it has been done.

Linna had succeeded to perfection.

"Who would have thought it possible for one so young as she to learn the trick?" Ben asked himself. "I have tried it many a time without the bone, but never could do it."

He looked at her admiringly, and was certain she was the smartest girl he had ever seen.

"If there are any turkeys within hearing, that is bound to fetch them, but I have seen no signs of them."

Linna continued the signalling at intervals for fifteen minutes or more, peeping meanwhile from behind the tree and around her in every direction. Ben did the same, and saw nothing.

"Why don't shoot?" she abruptly asked.

He noted the direction of her gaze, and there, not fifty feet away, was a big hen turkey, walking slowly over the leaves, with head aloft and glancing here and there for the lost one.

The target was a good one, and taking careful aim, Ben toppled it fluttering to the ground at the first fire.

"Dat all want?" queried Linna.

"Yes; that will do for tonight, Linna."

"Den go back—play wid Alice."

And off she ran to rejoin her companion, while the delighted lad picked up his prize and brought it to camp.

Turning that and his knife over to his mother, he made a fire ready to pass the night, full of thankfulness that all had gone so well. Ben agreed to stand watch until near midnight, and then allow his mother to help him at the necessary duty.

While the simple preparations were going on, Linna knelt on the bare ground with her ear pressed to the earth. Almost instantly she raised her head and whispered:

"Somebody comin' dis way—guess be Injins!"

CHAPTER NINE: IN A CIRCLE

This was alarming news. Ben Ripley imitated the action of Linna. Kneeling down, he pressed his ear to the earth.

Yes; he heard faint footfalls. Persons were moving about not far away.

"She is right," he said in a low tone; "likely they are Indians, though we cannot be certain."

"It won't do to wait till they come to us," remarked his mother.

"Shall I put out the fire?" asked Ben, disconcerted by the suddenness of the danger.

"No; we can't spare the time. Let us leave. Come, children."

She took the hand of each girl and walked quickly off, while Ben caught up the blankets and followed. They had no particular point in view, but wished to reach a safe place without delay.

The gloom of the gathering night helped them, and when they paused they were confident they had not been seen by anyone.

Without any thought on their part, they made their way to a mass of rocks and boulders, more extensive than any seen through the day. It was a hundred yards from their starting point.

They sat down for a whispered consultation.

"They must have heard the report of my rifle," said Ben.

"That was a considerable while ago, and they may have been a good way off at the time."

"Then, being so much nearer, it was the report which brought them. What would become of us but for Linna?" added Ben placing his arm affectionately around her. "It was she that got us our supper, and now she warns us of danger."

"They may be Zitner and Burwink."

"Not likely, but if they come to our fire we shall soon find out. Look!"

To their astonishment, the little fire which they had left only a few minutes before burned up brightly, showing that a lot of fuel had been thrown on it.

Too many trees and too much undergrowth obtruded for them to detect anything more than the great increase in brightness.

"The darkness will prevent their following our footprints," whispered the mother.

"I will go a little nearer and find out what it means: it may be, after all, that they are friends."

"Be careful, my son."

"I will."

It was not a hard task Ben Ripley gave himself. He had not far to go, and he proceeded with so much caution that no risk was involved. Only half the distance was passed when he gained a full view of the camp fire and its surroundings.

The sight was disquieting. Three Indian warriors were there. One had been gathering dry sticks which he flung on the blaze; another was helping himself to what was left of the cooked turkey; while the third, bent low, moved slowly around the lit up portion of the ground with his eyes fixed on it.

It was plain he was scrutinizing the footprints made by the party that had left just in time to escape them. It was a fortunate discovery made by Linna!

With the aid of the bright glare, it could not take him long to identify the little party as fugitives fleeing eastward, though it may be questioned whether they learned that it consisted of one large boy, an adult woman, and two small children.

They were in the battle yesterday. They have left others to look after those in Wyoming, while they are hunting the poor creatures that have taken to the woods.

The Iroquois who had been studying the ground straightened himself up and said something to the others. One of them then flung more fuel on the flames, and he who was ravenously eating suspended his operations, but quickly resumed again, as if he liked his occupation better than anything else to which he could turn his attention.

Then the first stooped down and caught up a burning brand. Several quick circles over his head fanned it into a vigorous blaze. Holding it aloft, with his shoulders bent forward, he moved slowly towards Ben Ripley.

He was tracing the footprints by the aid of the torch!

"Gracious! he will be among us in a minute," was the terrifying thought of the lad, who turned and ran back to his friends, in such haste that he was in danger of betraying his movements.

"Leave—quick!" he said; "they are after us!"

"No, they are not," replied his mother, who nevertheless stood ready to do as he said.

Ben looked back. The warrior with a torch, after walking a rod or so from the fire, had stopped, and was now in plain sight, with the flaming brand held above his head, while he peered out in the gloom in the direction of the fugitives, as if expecting to discern them.

Could he have known how near they were, he and his companions would have rushed down upon them; but they must have thought they had fled much further. It was impossible to trail them by torchlight as fast as they could travel, and the Indians did not waste time in the effort. The one with the torch went back to his companions.

The incident warned our friends of a new form of danger, which until then had not been counted among the probabilities.

The Indians, as you know, can trace a person through the woods with wonderful skill, seeing signs where the untrained eye observes nothing. If these three chose to wait where they were until daylight, there was nothing to prevent their taking up the trail and tracing the fugitives wherever they went.

"It won't do to stay here," said Ben, "for they will be right upon us at daylight."

"Providing they wait where they are."

"Why should they not do so? They are looking for us."

Mrs. Ripley dared not answer the question as her heart prompted. At the same time, she could think of no means of throwing them off their track.

"It might have been better had we stayed with Zitner and Burwink—no, it would not have been," she corrected herself, "for they were unfriendly to Linna. But we must go."

The only hope that presented itself was that they might travel so far during the darkness that the Indians would not keep up the pursuit when the trail was revealed to them.

The moon did not rise until very late, and there being no path, while all were in total ignorance of the neighborhood, it will be understood that they had set to work to do a very hard, if not impossible thing.

Ben as usual took the lead, and, before he had gone twenty steps, was caught under the chin by a protruding limb that almost lifted him off his feet. Then he went headlong into a hollow and bruised himself against some stones. Still, he did not give up, and by and by the ground became more level and his mishaps less frequent.

Alice and Linna, like little heroines, never murmured. All persevered until it was agreed that they were at least two miles from the camp fire.

In making this hard journey, every one of the party met with several narrow escapes, and it was agreed that it was best to go no further until daylight.

"As soon as we can see, we'll be off again, and ought to be able to travel as fast as they will do. Where they must watch all the time for our footprints, they cannot go off a walk."

"We may as well wait."

Throughout their haste, the blankets had been preserved. Indeed, the one over Ben's arm had served to break his fall more than once. These were placed on the ground, and the children lay down beside each other, quickly sinking to sleep; but the others, though pretty well worn, were too anxious to rest yet awhile.

"I have no idea where we are," said the son; "but one place is as good as another at such a time, and the weather is so warm that blankets are not needed. Now, mother, I wish you would lie down beside the children and rest. You need it badly, I know."

"And so do you, my son."

"Not for some time yet."

"But, if you intend to watch until daylight, you will be worn out by morning. Besides, you cannot stay awake unless you move about. I will agree to lie down if you will promise to call me when you think it is midnight, and let me take a turn."

"I will agree to call you when I feel the need of you, and I will pace the ground like a sentinel on duty."

The mother was forced to accept this proposition and, after some more cautious conversation, she did as her boy wished, and he was left alone.

Ben did not forget his slip of the night before. It was necessary that one of the company should maintain watch while the others slept, and only these two could do it. He meant to guard the others through the short summer night, trusting to a chance of getting what slumber he needed on the morrow when the others were awake.

"I would like to catch myself waking her," he mused, after he had groped around until he found a space a couple of rods in length over which he could pace back and forth.

Then, with his rifle resting on his shoulder, he began his patient beat, surrounded by impenetrable gloom, and with the lives of three loved ones in his keeping.

By and by a lighting of the sky showed the moon had risen. This, however, was of little or no help, since the abundance of leaves prevented its rays piercing between and lighting up the ground beneath.

It would be hard to imagine a more gloomy occupation than that of Ben Ripley while engaged with this duty. The solemn murmur of the vast woods around him, the world of darkness in which he slowly paced to and fro, the memory of the sad scenes he had seen in the lovely Wyoming Valley, the certainty that a good many miles must yet be traversed before they could sit down in safety, the consciousness that several of the cruel red men were near them, and the belief that they would start in pursuit as soon as it was light—all this oppressed him with crushing weight, and made him feel at times as if there was no escape for him and his loved ones.

"There is only one way of hiding our trail," he mused. "If we could come upon some river or large stream of water, where there was a boat, or we could make a raft, we should be safe. A big rainstorm would do as well, for it would wash out all signs of our footprints."

He paused in his walk and peeped up at a speck of sky shown through a rift among the limbs.

"There is hardly a cloud; it looks as if it wouldn't rain for a week, and I don't know of any river between here and the Delaware."

His senses were never more alert. He avoided the fatal mistake of sitting down for a few minutes, or so much as leaning against a tree to rest. He stopped, however, now and then and listened intently.

"I wonder whether I am mistaken, or whether I did hear something moving over the leaves out there?"

The fact that the almost inaudible rustling was noticed only when he himself was in motion inclined him to suspect it was a delusion, accounted for by his tense nerves. But after a time he became certain of a fact hardly less startling in its nature.

When walking back and forth with his face away from the spot where his friends lay something gleamed a short distance off among the trees. Its location showed it was on the ground, and, as nearly as he could judge, less than a hundred feet off.

His first supposition was that it was a fungus growth known in the country as "foxfire," which gives out a phosphorescent glow in the darkness; but after watching and studying it for a long time, he was convinced it was something else.

"I'm going to find out," he decided; "it won't take me long, and I ought to know all about it, for it may concern us."

Stealing forward, he was not a little astonished to find it a real fire, sunken to a glowing ember, left by someone.

"It must be as Zitner said—the woods are full of Indians, and some of them have camped there."

Not wishing to stumble over any of their bodies, he manoeuvred until assured that whoever kindled the fire had left, when he kicked aside the ashes.

The act caused a twist of flame to spring up and throw out a tiny glare, which illumined several feet of surrounding space.

And then the astonished youth made the discovery that this was the very spot where they had cooked their turkey hours before, and from which they had fled in hot haste before the approach of the three Iroquois.

He and his friends had travelled in a circle, and come back to their starting point.

CHAPTER TEN: NEAR THE END

Anyone who is used to the woods knows how apt he is to wander in a circle unless he keeps his wits about him. There have been many causes named for this curious fact, and the one that strikes me as the most reasonable is that we are all either right or left handed. It is rare that you meet a person who is ambidextrous,—that is, who uses both hands equally well. When, therefore, he sets out to travel through the woods without any guide, he unconsciously exerts his right or left limb, as the case may be, more than the other, and this makes his course circular.

There are three "signboards" by which a hunter can keep trace of the points of the compass when in the woods, without noticing the sun, which of itself is often a great help. Three fourths of the moss on trees grows on the north side; the heaviest boughs on spruce trees are always on the south side, and the topmost twig of every uninjured hemlock tree tips to the east.

Now, while these signs never err, you can see that it is almost impossible to turn them to account at night.

Ben Ripley had led his friends in an irregular circle, and brought them back to within a brief distance of the starting point. This was the camp fire from which they fled in such panic before the approach of the three red men.

The discovery filled him with dismay, and he darted out in the darkness for the rocks where the others were sleeping. His first intention was to rouse them and plunge into the woods again, but a few minutes served to make him cooler and more collected in mind.

The night was well spent, and a flight of that kind could not do much for them. It might be all in vain. It would be trying to the last degree. He decided not to disturb the sleepers.

By and by he persuaded himself that matters were not as bad as they first appeared. Inasmuch as the fugitives had not returned over their own trail, the Indians, in case they took it in the morning, must make the same circuit, and thus be forced to go just as far as if the flight had been in a direct line.

It was a mystery, however, what had become of the three warriors. They could not be near the camp, or they would have appeared when the lad returned to it. They had left, but who could say whither they had gone?

While Ben was debating the painful question, a growing light in the direction of the Delaware told him the night was ended and the new day dawning.

The fourth day of July, the second anniversary of the Declaration of Independence, had passed. He thought of it, standing alone in the dismal forest with danger on every hand, and oppressed by the great fear that those whom he loved more than his own life must perish in that gloomy wilderness.

He did not dare, however, to give way to his sad thoughts. At the first streakings of light among the trees, he roused his mother and told her the alarming truth.

"I do not understand it," she replied, alluding to the absence of the Iroquois; "it must be they are in the neighborhood."

The children were still sleeping quietly on the blanket. No food or water was at command, and they could not take the time to look for any. Indeed, the two elder ones felt no hunger or thirst.

The mother rose to her feet and looked around, her interest centring on the rock and boulders, which stretched away to the rear further than they could penetrate with the eye.

"I know they are skilful in following footprints," she remarked; "but if we walk carefully over those rocks, I think they will not be able to track us. We will try it."

The children were roused and quickly learned what was to be done, the mother adding that the prayer which she was accustomed to offer up every morning would be given when they reached a spot where it was safe to do so.

For fully a hundred yards the four were able to make their way without resting their feet on the ground. Then the boulders ended as abruptly as they began.

All now kneeled on the granite floor and asked Heaven to deliver them safely out of the dangers by which they were surrounded.

If the Indians chose to make search, after tracing the little party to the stony place, they must eventually come upon the new trail, where it began again on the ground; but unless they struck it by accident, they must use a good deal of time in hunting for it.

"Come on," called Ben in a low voice, but with a renewal of hope; "we shall get somewhere one of these days."

To their surprise, not far from the rocks they came upon a faintly marked path among the trees.

"What is the meaning of that?" Ben asked, looking inquiringly at his mother and Linna.

"Men don't do dat—wild beasts," replied the dusky child.

"She is right," added the mother; "the animals follow it to water; let us do the same."

The haunting fear of the red men made the words between the fugitives few, and all their movements guarded. They kept glancing to right and left, in front and to the rear, Linna being probably the most active. It was as if she inherited from her parents their surprising woodcraft, and was now calling it into play for the benefit of her friends.

Suddenly something flickered in the path ahead, and Ben stopped short, those behind him doing the same.

Just in advance—less than fifty yards indeed—a beautiful fawn had come to a halt. Its graceful head, with its soft brown eyes, was lifted high, and it looked wonderingly at the people, as if not knowing the meaning, and too innocent to feel fear. Ben drew up his rifle, for it was a tempting chance for a delicious breakfast. But almost instantly he lowered the weapon again.

The fawn was so trusting, so unsuspicious, that a feeling of pity came to the young hunter. The animal suggested his own little sister, for it was wandering through the unfriendly woods, with none to protect it from cruel enemies.

"Go," whispered Ben; "I haven't the heart to harm you; I will starve first."

"Remember the result of the shot yesterday," said his mother warningly. "We are in too much peril to increase it."

The lad advanced along the path, and every one of the company smiled at the fawn, when it stood motionless, staring until they were almost to it. Then the timid creature turned nimbly and trotted over the trail, its head so high that, as it turned it from side to side, it saw every thing done by the strange beings following.

Had the situation been less serious, Ben would have had some sport with the lovely creature, but he dared not give it much attention. It continued trotting a short way, and then sprang gracefully aside among the trees, leaving no scent on the leaves by which the most highly trained hound could trace it.

A little way beyond they came upon the largest stream seen since leaving the mountains east of the Susquehanna. It was a dozen feet in width, quite deep, rapid, and clear.

"Here is enough drink for us all," said Ben, and they proceeded to help themselves in the primitive fashion described elsewhere.

"That must contain fish," observed the mother; "but we are without the means of catching them."

"Unless Linna will jump in and haul them out for us. But if we are to continue our journey, we must find some way of getting to the other side; it is too deep and wide to ford or jump."

"It must be narrower in other places."

"Oh! look mamma!"

It was Alice who first saw a terrifying sight. An immense black bear, the largest any of the party had ever seen, swung from among the trees and came to the water's edge on the other side.

He was so enormous that all started and recoiled a step, even Linna uttering an exclamation in her own tongue. Ben grasped his rifle, and held it ready to use the instant it became necessary.

But Bruin was in a gracious mood that morning. He looked at the party with stupid curiosity, then reared on his hind legs, and swung his beam-.like paws in an odd way.

"He is inviting us to come over and be hugged to death," laughed Ben.

"He will come over and eat us all up," said Alice, clinging to the dress of her mother.

"No," replied the parent, soothingly patting her head; "Ben won't let him do that. Do not be frightened."

"Climb tree," suggested Linna; "not big tree, 'cause bear climb dat too—climb little tree, den he can't climb it."

"You are right, but we will wait and see what he does. I don't want to fire my gun unless I have to, and if he will let us alone we won't hurt him. There! he is going to drink."

The huge creature bent his head down to the water and helped himself. When he had had enough, he raised his snout and again looked at the party, who were closely watching him.

This was the critical moment. If he meant to attack them, he would plunge into the water and either swim or wade across. Ben raised the hammer of his rifle and awaited his action.

Had Bruin been hungry, he would not have dallied so long; but he did not seem to see anything specially tempting in the group, and lumbered off among the trees.

"A lucky move for you." remarked Ben.

"And just as lucky for us," added the mother; "for though you might have slain him, as I have no doubt you would, the report of the gun must have brought more dangerous enemies to us."

"I would give a good deal to know what has become of them. It begins to look as if they did not consider us worth bothering with."

"I wish I could believe that, but I cannot. I think it more likely that they know where we are, and are trifling with us, as a cat does with a mouse."

"That makes me anxious to push on. We must find some place where we can cross the stream. Let's go further up the bank."

He took the course named, leading away from the great bear with which they had so narrowly escaped an encounter.

To their surprise, they had not far to go before the spot they were seeking was found. The stream narrowed between some rocks, so much that even Alice could spring across without wetting her feet.

"I am afraid Linna can't leap it," remarked Ben with a smile.

"Me show you."

And, without recoiling a step, the nimble little one made a graceful bound, which landed her several feet beyond the other margin.

"Well done!" said Ben; "I couldn't do much better myself. Now, Alice, you are not going to let her beat you?"

Alice was timid at first, but with a good start she cleared the space. She landed, however, so near the water that had not the watchful Linna caught one of the hands thrown up to save herself, she would have fallen back in the stream.

Mother and son imitated them, and all stood on the other side of the obstruction without having suffered any inconvenience.

While they were congratulating themselves, a startling reminder of their danger came in the near report of a rifle. It was from the direction in which they had seen the bear, and in the stillness of the woods all heard a snarling growl, which proved that the beast had received his death wound.

"The Indians are there!" whispered the frightened Ben; "what shall we do, mother?"

"What can we do?" she asked, helpless and at her wits' end for the moment; "there seems to be no escaping them."

"Me go talk with them," was the amazing remark of the little Delaware girl.

"You talk with them!" repeated Mrs. Ripley; "what can you do?"

"Don't know—me try."

And without waiting for permission, Linna started on a light run toward the point whence came the report of the rifle that gave Bruin his death wound. Mother and son looked in each other's face in mute wonderment for a full minute after the departure of the girl.

"She's a remarkable child," finally said the mother; "she has done us more than one good turn, and, it may be, Heaven intends to make use of her again, though I cannot see how."

"The Iroquois will recognise her as one of their own race. Perhaps one or more of them belong to her tribe: they will know her as the child of Omas, and may listen to her pleadings."

"Alas! they will give little heed to them; my heart misgives me, son: I feel that the end is at hand."

Meanwhile, let us follow Linna, the Delaware, upon her strange mission.

CHAPTER ELEVEN: ALL IN VAIN

I am at some disadvantage in giving an account of the remarkable interview between the little Delaware girl, Linna, and the three hostile warriors who had trailed the Ripleys to the stream in the wilderness across which they had just leaped in the effort to continue their flight from Wyoming to the Upper Delaware.

There were no witnesses to the interview except the parties named, but when Linna in after years had become a woman, with her very strong memory she gave a description of what passed, and it has come down through the descendants of the pioneers to the present day.

You will permit me to found my narrative upon her testimony, and to be quite liberal in the interpretation of what took place.

The fears of the fugitives were well founded. The three red men were near them for a long while before they showed themselves. It was very much as Mrs. Ripley had said. They were so sure of the prize that they trifled with them.

Linna reached the spot where the warriors were standing directly after one of the number had sent a bullet through the bear. Young as she was, she understood the peril of her friends, and set out to do all she could for them.

She knew that Omas, her father, was a great warrior. He belonged to the Delaware tribe, which years before had been soundly beaten by the Iroquois and reduced almost to slavery; but among the conquered people were many without superiors in bravery, skill, and prowess. Omas was one of the most noted examples.

The first thrill of hope came to the young child when she recognised the one that had killed the bear. He was Red Wolf, a member of her own tribe, who often had been in her father's wigwam, and was therefore well known to his child. The others were of the Seneca tribe, one of those composing the Iroquois, or Six Nations, the most powerful confederation of Indians that ever existed on the American continent.

The three looked at the little girl in amazement, as she came running between the trees. She dropped to a rapid walk, and did not stop until she was among them.

"Where do you come from?" asked Red Wolf, in the Delaware tongue.

"My father, the great Omas, brought me to see my friend Alice. He left me with her people, and you must not harm them."

"Why did Omas leave you with them?"

"They are my friends."

It should be said the Senecas, who calmly listened to the conversation, understood all that was said.

"Where are you going?"

"A long way through the wood."

"Why does Omas leave you with the palefaces? You should be in your own wigwam many miles away."

"He knows I am safe with them. He led us through the woods until he could leave us; then he went back to the great river between the mountains to help the other warriors fight."

None of the three could doubt that the child was speaking the truth. They held the prowess of Omas in high respect; but they were not the ones to surrender such a prize as was already theirs.

"We will take them back to Wyoming with us," said Red Wolf; "then Omas may do as he thinks best with them."

With a shrewdness far beyond her years, Linna said—"He wants them to go to the other big river, off yonder"—pointing eastward. "Why do you wish to take them back to Wyoming?"

"If he wants them to go to the other big river, he can send them after he sees them again."

"You will make Omas angry; he will strike you down with his tomahawk," said Linna.

Although these words were the words of a child, they produced their effect. Red Wolf knew how deeply the grim warrior loved his only daughter, and he knew, too, how terrible was the wrath of the warrior. Omas had chosen to spare this family from the cruelty visited upon so many others. If Red Wolf dared to run the risk of rousing the vengeance of Omas, he must take the consequences. He shrank from doing so.

The Delaware beckoned to one of the Senecas, and they stepped aside and talked a few minutes, in tones too low for the listening Linna to hear what was said. Subsequent events, however, made clear the meaning of their conversation.

Red Wolf proposed to spare the fugitives. He wished to go away with his companions and leave them to pursue their flight without molestation, so far as they were concerned.

But the Senecas held Omas in less dread than did Red Wolf. They were unwilling to let the whites escape. The third warrior, who joined them, was as strenuous as the first. While one might have shrunk from stirring the anger of the famous Delaware, the two together did not hesitate to run counter to his wishes. They refused to be dissuaded by Red Wolf.

They remained apart from the girl for ten minutes, earnestly conversing, while she could not overhear a word.

Finally one of the three—a Seneca—turned about and walked away, as if impatient with the dispute. He took a course leading from the stream, and deeper into the woods.

Linna noticed the curious act, but, great as was her acumen for one of her years, she did not suspect its meaning. It would have been passing strange had she done so, for the movement was meant to deceive her and bring the disputation to an end.

The couple remaining walked to where Linna awaited them. The Seneca turned aside and sauntered to the carcass of the bear as if that had more interest just then for him.

"What will Omas do if my brother warriors take your friends back to the other river, but Red Wolf does not help?"

"He will strike them down with his tomahawk; my father, Omas, is a great warrior."

The black eyes flashed as the girl proudly uttered these words, and she looked defiantly in the painted face towering above her.

"But what will he do with Red Wolf?"

"He will strike down Red Wolf, because he is a coward, and did not keep all harm from his white friends."

This intimation that the Delaware could not shelter himself behind the plea of neutrality, but must be either an active friend or foe, was a little more than he could accept. While he held Omas in wholesome dread, he dared not array himself against the two Senecas, who were determined not to spare the hapless fugitives.

Red Wolf was a fair specimen of his tribe, who, as I have stated, were beaten by the Iroquois. These conquerors, indeed, carried matters with so high a hand that they once forbade the Delawares to use firearms, but made them keep to the old fashioned bow and arrow.

Red Wolf, therefore, having squared accounts, so to speak, with his present companions, was anxious to win the good will of Linna, and thereby that of her fierce parent, who was a hurricane in his wrath, and likely to brain Red Wolf before he could explain matters.

"Omas is the greatest warrior of the Delawares," he said to Linna; "Red Wolf and he are brothers. But the Senecas will not listen to the words of Red Wolf: they love not Omas as does Red Wolf."

The Delaware child now found herself in a quandary. She had made her plea, but, so far as she could see, it was in vain, since the friendship of Red Wolf alone was not enough. One of the Senecas was studying the body of the dead bear and paying no heed to her words; the other had gone off, she knew not where.

What remained for her to do?

While the little one asked herself the question, and was trying, to think what course she should follow, the absent Seneca was working out the mischievous plot he had formed, and which was fully known to his companions.

An uprooted tree lay extended on the ground, near where Mrs. Ripley and her children saw Linna run off to plead with the Indians. Since they could do nothing but wait, helpless and almost despairing, for the return of the child, they sat down on the prostrate trunk.

Ben was near the base, close to the mass of upturned roots, which spread out like an enormous fan, with its dirt and prong-like roots projecting in all directions. He was tired, depressed, and worn out. It will be remembered he had not slept a wink during the preceding night, or eaten a mouthful of food since then. Strong, sturdy, and lusty as he was, he could not help feeling the effects of all this.

He leaned his rifle against a huge, gnarled root, within arm's length of where he half reclined, with his feet extended along the trunk. He had but to reach out his hand, without moving his body, to grasp the weapon whatever moment it might be needed.

Exhausted as he was, his condition was too nervous to permit slumber. His mother had said she thought the end was at hand, and he believed the same.

She was but a few feet away, sitting more erect on the tree, with Alice leaning against her.

The eyes of all were turned toward the point where Linna had vanished, and whence she was expected every minute to come into view again.

She was not far off. Once or twice the mother and son caught the sounds of their voices, though the exuberant vegetation shut them from sight.

"It was idle for her to go," said Ben; "and I cannot see any chance of her helping us."

"They will not harm her, nor will they be denied the pleasure of doing what they choose with us."

"Some persons might believe the delay was favorable, but I cannot think that way."

Neither felt like conversation. It was an effort to say anything; but mother and son, in their unselfishness, pitied each other, and strove vainly to lift the gloomy thoughts that were oppressing both.

Had Ben Ripley seen the departure of the Seneca, he might have suspected its meaning; but, unaware of it, he never dreamed of the new form which the ever present danger thus assumed.

The Seneca, after leaving Red Wolf and the other warrior, walked directly over the path leading away from the stream until well beyond the sight of those thus left behind. He looked back, and, seeing nothing of them, turned aside and moved off, until he arrived at a point beyond the group of three resting on the fallen tree.

Thus, as will be seen, the Ripleys were between the two and Linna on the one hand, and the single Seneca on the other. He knew the precise location of the fugitives as well as if they had been in his field of vision from the first.

He now began approaching them from the rear. Their faces turned away from him, and everything favored his stealthy advance.

The huge spread of dirt and roots made by the overturning of the big tree served as a screen, though even without this help he would probably have succeeded in his effort to steal upon them unawares.

He stepped so carefully upon the dried leaves that no sound was made, and the most highly trained ear, therefore, would not have detected him.

If Ben had once risen from his reclining posture and looked around, if Mrs. Ripley had stood up and done the same, or if little Alice had indulged in her natural sportiveness, assuredly one of them would have observed that crouching warrior, gradually drawing closer, like the moving of a hand over the face of a clock; but none saw him. Nearer and nearer he came, step by step, until at last he stood just on the other side of the mass of roots, and not ten feet from the boy.

With the same noiselessness, the crouching form bent over sideways and peered around the screen. Then the dusky arm glided forward until the iron fingers clasped the barrel of the rifle leaning against the root, and the weapon was withdrawn.

He now had two guns, and Ben Ripley none.

Then the Seneca advanced, a weapon in either hand, and, presenting himself in front of the amazed group, exclaimed—"Huh! how do, bruder?—how do sister?"

Ben Ripley sprang up as if shot, and his startled mother, with a gasp of affright, turned her head.

For one moment the boy meditated leaping upon the warrior, in the desperate attempt to wrench his gun from his grasp; but the mother, reading his intention, interposed.

"Do nothing, my son: we are in the hands of Heaven."

CHAPTER TWELVE: CONCLUSION

The point, at last, had been reached where it was useless to struggle any longer. The little party of fugitives, after safely crossing the Susquehanna on the day of the battle, and penetrating more than a score of miles on their way eastward to the Delaware, were overtaken, and made captive by three Indians.

Warning Ben against any resistance, the mother bowed her head in submission, and awaited her fate. Only once, when she clasped her arm around the awed and silent Alice, laying the other affectionately upon the shoulder of her brave son, did she speak—"Murmur not at the will of Heaven."

The Seneca was surprised at the action, or, rather, want of action, on the part of the captives. Receiving no response to his salutation, he stood a moment in silence, and then emitted a tremulous whoop. It was a signal for Red Wolf and the other Seneca. They understood it, and hurried to the spot, with Linna close behind them.

It would have been expected that she would indulge in some outburst when she saw how ill everything had gone; but, with one grieved look, she went up to the sorrowing, weeping mother and buried her head between her knees.

And then she did what no one of that party had ever before seen her do—she sobbed with a breaking heart. The mother soothed her as best she could, uttering words which she heard not.

Ben Ripley when the blow came, stood erect, and folded his arms. His face was pale, but his lips were mute. Not even by look did he ask for mercy from their captors.

In the midst of the impressive tableau, Linna suddenly raised her head from the lap of the mother, her action and attitude showing she had caught some sound which she recognized.

But everyone else in the party also noted it. It was a shrill, penetrating whistle, ringing among the forest arches—a call which she had heard many a time, and she could never mistake its meaning.

Her eyes sparkled through her tears, which wet her cheeks; but she forgot everything but that signal.

"Dat Omas!—dat Omas—dat fader!" she exclaimed, springing to her feet, trembling and aglow with excitement.

There was one among the three who, had his painted complexion permitted, would have turned ashy pale. Red Wolf was afraid that when the fearful Delaware warrior thundered down on them, he would not give his brother time to explain matters before sinking his tomahawk into his brain. Manifestly, therefore, but one course was open for him, and he took it without a second's delay.

He fled for his life.

The Senecas, however, stood their ground. The signal of Omas sounded again, and Linna answered it. Her father was near at hand, and quickly came to view.

But, lo! he had a companion. It was To-wika, his faithful wife.

The reunion of the Delaware family was an extraordinary one. Had no others been present, Linna would have bounded into the arms of her mother, been pressed impulsively to her breast, and then received the same fervent welcome from her father.

But never could anything like that take place before witnesses.

When the child saw her parents she walked gravely up to them, having first done her utmost to remove the traces of tears, and took her place by their side. The mother said something in her native tongue, but it could not have been of much account, for the child gave no reply.

Omas did not speak. One quick glance was bestowed upon his child, and then he addressed himself to the work before him.

Omas was as cunning as a serpent. He would not have hesitated to assail these two Senecas, for, truth to tell, he could never feel much love for the conquerors of his people. He did not fear them; but he saw the way to win his point without such tempestuous violence.

His words, therefore, were calculated to soothe rather than irritate. He asked them to explain how it was they were in charge of his friends, and listened attentively while one of them answered his inquiry.

Then, as is natural with his race, he recounted in somewhat extravagant language his own deeds of the last few days. There is reason to believe he gave himself credit for a number of exploits against the palefaces of which he was innocent.

Then he said the only ones he loved among the palefaces were the three there present—he had entrusted his only child to them, and they had saved her from the anger of their people. He had slept under their roof, and eaten of their bread. They were his best friends; and they his brave Seneca brothers, when they knew of this, would be glad. He had set out to conduct them to the settlements, and his brothers would wish all a safe arrival there.

This speech, delivered with far more address than I am able to give it, worked as a charm. Not the slightest reference was made to the cowardly Red Wolf, though Omas knew all about him.

The Senecas were won by the words of the wily Delaware. They indulged in the fiction of saying that they had no thought of how matters stood between him and these palefaces, and their hearts were glad to hear the words fall from his lips. They would not harm his friends, and hoped they would reach in safety the settlement for which they were looking.

Not only that, but they offered to go with them all the way.

This was too kind, and the offer was gratefully declined. Then the Senecas withdrew, first returning Ben's rifle to him. Whether they ever succeeded in overtaking Red Wolf cannot be known, and it is of no moment.

The peril had burst over the heads of the little party like a thundercloud; and now it had cleared, and all was sunshine again.

It was some minutes before the Ripleys could fully understand the great good fortune that had come to them. Then their hearts overflowed with thankfulness.

With her arms clasping her children Mrs. Ripley looked devoutly upward, and murmured:

"I thank Thee, Heavenly Father, for Thy great mercy to me and mine. Bless Omas and To-wika and Linna, and hold them for ever in Thy precious keeping."

The events which had taken place were strange; but Mrs. Ripley maintained, to the end of her life, that those which followed were tenfold more remarkable.

You will remember that when Omas, after conducting the little company some distance from Wyoming, showed a wish to leave them, the good woman had no doubt what his purpose was: he wanted to take part in further cruelties against the hapless settlers.

Omas had fought hard in the battle of July 3rd, 1778, and his friendship for the Ripleys drew him away before the dreadful doings were half completed. He yearned to go back and give rein to his ferocity. Mrs. Ripley tried to restrain him, but in vain.

Such were her views; but she was in error. She did not read the heart of the terrible warrior aright.

For weeks Omas had been sorely troubled in mind. He had visited the Christian brethren of his own tribe at the Moravian settlement of Gnadenhutten. He had listened to the talk of the missionaries, and heard of One who, when He was reviled, reviled not again; who, when He was smitten and spat upon, bore it meekly; and who finally died on the cross, that the red men as well as the white children might be saved.

All this was a great mystery to the Delaware. He could not grasp the simple but sublime truths which lie at the foundation of Christianity. But he longed to do so. At midnight he lay trying to sleep in the silent woods, looking up at the stars and meditating on the wonderful Being who had done all this. In the simplicity of his nature, he talked to that awful and dimly comprehended Father of all races and peoples, and asked Him to tell Omas what he should say, and do, and think.

Unknown to him, To-wika his wife had listened to the teachings of the missionaries, and she had traversed further along the path of light than he.

When, therefore, he told her of his longings, his questionings, his distress, his wretchedness, and his groping in the dark, she was able to say a great deal that helped to clear away the fogs and mists from his clouded brain.

But Omas was in the very depth of darkness, and almost despair, when the fearful episode of Wyoming came. It was in desperation he went into that conflict, as a man will sometimes do to escape, as it were, from himself.

He fought like a demon, but he could not hush the still small voice within his breast. He felt that he must have relief, or he would do that which a wild Indian never does—make away with himself.

It was on his tongue more than once, while threading his way through the wilderness with his friends, to appeal to Mrs. Ripley; but with a natural shrinking he held back, fearing that with his broken words he could not make her understand his misery.

The only recourse was to go to To-wika, his wife. He had asked her to talk further with the missionaries, and then to repeat their words to him.

So it was that when he stole from the camp fire like a thief in the night, it was not to return and take part in the scenes of violence in which he had already been so prominent an actor, but to do the very opposite.

It was a long tramp through the forest to his own wigwam, and his people were aflame with excitement because of Wyoming; but the warrior hardly paused night and day until he flung himself at the feet of To-wika and begged that he might die.

From this remarkable woman Linna had inherited more mental strength than from her iron hearted father. To-wika talked soothingly to him, and for the first time in his blind groping he caught a glimmer of light. The blessed Word which had brought comfort and happiness to her is for all people and conditions, no matter how rude, how ignorant, and how fallen.

But To-wika felt the need of human help. She had never met Mrs. Ripley, but her husband had told of his welcome beneath that roof, and of what she said to him about the Saviour and God, who was so different from the Great Spirit of the red men. She knew this woman was a Christian, and she asked her husband to lead her to her.

He set out with her to overtake the little party who, with never a thought of what was going on, were struggling through the gloomy wilderness, beset by perils on every hand.

Since they were following no beaten path, except for a little way, the most perfect woodcraft was necessary to find them. Omas knew the direction they had taken, and calculated the time needed to reach the Delaware. It was easy, too, to locate the camp where he had parted from them, after which his wonderful skill enabled him to keep the trail, along which he and his wife strode with double the speed of the fugitives.

When he discovered that three warriors were doing the same, all the old fire and wrath flamed up in his nature. The couple increased the ardor of their pursuit. And yet, but for the favoring aid of Heaven, they hardly could have come up at the crisis which brought them all together.

Under the blest instruction of Mrs. Ripley, the doubts of Omas finally vanished, never to return. The once mighty warrior, foremost in battle and ferocity and courage, became the meek, humble follower of the Saviour—triumphant in life, and doubly triumphant in death.

On the third day after the meeting in the woods, the party arrived at the little town of Stroudsburg, on the Upper Delaware, none having suffered the least harm. The skill of Omas kept them supplied with food, and his familiarity with the route did much to lessen the hardships which otherwise they would have suffered.

Omas stayed several weeks at this place with his friends, and then he and his wife and little one joined the Christian settlement of Gnadenhutten, where the couple finished their days.

After a time, when it became safe for the Ripleys to return to Wyoming Valley, they took up their residence there once more, and remained until the husband and father came back at the close of the Revolution; and the happy family were reunited, thankful that God had been so merciful to them and brought independence to their beloved country.

Omas and To-wika and Linna were welcome visitors as long as the lived. In truth, Linna survived them all. She married a chieftain among her own people, and when she at last was gathered to her final rest, she had almost reached the great age of a hundred years.

13567089R00045

Printed in Great Britain
by Amazon.co.uk, Ltd.,
Marston Gate.